NORMAN SNODGRASS SAVES THE GREEN PLANET

NORMAN SNODGRASS
SAVES THE GREEN
PLANET

Written and Illustrated by

Sue Bough

Matador
9 Priory Business Park,
Wistow Road, Kibworth Beauchamp,
Leicestershire, LE8 0RX
Tel: 0116 279 2299
Email: books@troubador.co.uk
Web: www.troubador.co.uk/matador
Twitter: @matadorbooks

ISBN 978 1789018 783

British Library Cataloguing in Publication Data.
A catalogue record for this book is available from the British Library.

Printed and bound by CPI Group (UK) Ltd, Croydon, CR0 4YY
Typeset in 12pt Giovanni by Troubador Publishing Ltd, Leicester, UK

Matador is an imprint of Troubador Publishing Ltd

Heartfelt thanks to my family & friends who badgered me to bring Norman to life and who believed in him before a single word was written… For Pops, who will always be my Arthur Snodgrass – and for Charlie, my immovable rock.

CONTENTS

Look up at the sky on a winter's night and find Orion, the Hunter, with his twinkling belt of three stars. Follow their path to Sirius, the Dog Star, shining brighter than a thousand candles...

Stare long enough at Sirius and you'll see the ghostly outline of something else hidden there. Rub your eyes and it's gone – but it's no trick. Behind Sirius lies a secret planet, stranger than anything yet discovered... the Green Planet.

THE GREEN PLANET

FROM A DISTANCE, the Planet looked almost normal. Nothing strange about its craters that belched candyfloss-scented steam. Certainly nothing unusual about the rocks that lay quiet and still until… Wait a minute… Did that one just move?

Sure enough, a big rock opened a sleepy eye. It shook itself, sending a shower of sparkling dust into the air, then sneezed and settled back into its hollow.

Not such an ordinary place, after all.

The rock sat next to a large hole, lined with plastic tubing that poked out of the ground. Beside it was a post with a flashing sign that simply said 'Z'.

POFFFF!

Suddenly, the hole exploded.

The rock watched as something small and blue shot out and landed with a thump on its backside. As the dust cleared, the blue thing coughed and began to mutter.

POFFFF! Suddenly, the hole exploded.

"Blasted Zube Tubes... nearly choked me..."

The creature got up and dusted itself down. It pulled on a lead held in its three-fingered hand. The other end was attached to an excited ball of orange fluff.

"Come on, Spong... better get a move on. We've got to find these bugs before tea."

The blue object was in fact a Poggle called Norman Snodgrass. He had bright beady eyes, long pointy ears and a trumpet-shaped hooter instead of a nose. He wore only a belt, covered with many buttons, clips and lights, which squeezed his large stomach.

Norman waddled over to the rock and prodded it nervously with the longest of the three toes on his left foot. The rock opened its eye again, frowned and shuffled sideways. Norman sifted through the dust hollow... then jumped as something moved under his toes. He dived into a bag hanging from his belt. Pulling out a glass jar, he scooped up the dirt and screwed the lid shut.

Norman held up the jar. There was something whizzing around inside.

"Only a Double Bug but better than nothing," he sighed, watching a furious yellow insect with green spots buzzing and banging into the glass.

Without warning, it gave a loud 'PING!' and split into two identical bugs, which whirred around in opposite directions.

"Oh no... I should have collected this one last. There won't be room for anything else soon."

PING! Once again the Double Bug did what Double Bugs do best, and four insects now zoomed around, avoiding collision through split-second timing.

"Have to let 'em go, I suppose," Norman sighed. "Wouldn't impress Miss Lastic anyway; she only wants us to collect rare bugs. Nothing rare about these things..."

He shook the container glumly, setting off several more 'pings' and by the time he managed to open the jar, hundreds of Double Bugs scuttled off in a light green blur before burying themselves, bottoms first, in the dirt.

"Come on, Spong, better keep looking."

Norman ambled off while his furry companion poked its snout helpfully under the rocks and stones. A belch of steam erupted from a nearby crater. The animal sniffed the sweet air, whining to be let loose.

"Now, Spong," said Norman, "you know I can't do that. Strict instructions from Miss Lastic: *'Only let him off the lead indoors.'* I know what you'll do if I let you go!"

He rubbed Spong under the chin and the little creature turned from orange to a golden yellow. A series of squeaks and purrs followed, and Norman smiled, remembering the day they had first met.

"Right, Poggles," Norman's teacher had barked two weeks earlier, "shut down your Data-Globes and pay attention. We have been given a new pet to look after this term!"

Instantly the chat from Norman's classmates stopped. Everyone's attention was fixed on a metal box that was quivering slightly on Miss Lastic's desk. She opened it... and with the words, "This is Spong – he is a Reversible Minky..." she lifted out an orange ball that looked like a furry hedgehog. It squeaked excitedly in her hands. "Now, I'll pass him around so you can all stroke him," she continued, "but listen carefully to these instructions while you do so."

A tall, spotty Poggle quickly grabbed the creature from Miss Lastic's three-fingered hands.

"*Gently*, Boris Whinge!" she reprimanded.

The tall Poggle scowled and blushed.

"Now, Reversible Minkies are friendly animals that can be easily tamed," she began. "They are naturally curious and display their emotions through the colour of their fur. What you see now – orange – is their normal state. They turn pale orange when they sleep. Yellow means the Minky is happy, blue for sadness and purple means they're annoyed. They will turn white if they are frightened. They are also very useful in times of danger and will glow red as a warning."

The class of Poggles strained to get a glimpse of Spong, still held firmly in the clutches of Boris Whinge.

"There is one other colour," continued Miss Lastic. "Green, which means... Well, I'm sure we'll never see that. Now, Boris, pass Spong *carefully* to Ernie Sludgebucket – you've had him long enough."

Annoyed at being forced to give up the endearing pet, Boris threw him roughly to Ernie, who wasn't quite ready to catch him. There was a sharp intake of breath as Spong slipped from Ernie's grasp. Then the strangest thing happened...

In mid-air, before their astonished eyes, Spong flipped inside out! He became smooth and rubbery, like a ball, with four small paws and a snout, before hitting the ground with a *'Boiiiiinnnggg'* and bouncing gleefully off the walls, floor and ceiling.

Then the strangest thing happened...

Squeals of hysteria erupted from the Poggle class as they ran around trying to catch him.

"Calm down, calm *down!*" shouted Miss Lastic, dodging slightly as Spong whizzed past her left ear. "Now, if everyone will just sit down, I'll sort this mess out. This is exactly why I asked you to pass him *carefully*." She aimed a beady eye at Boris.

"Not my fault if Ernie can't catch," he muttered sulkily.

"The reason..." said Miss Lastic, ducking again as Spong rebounded over her head, "the reason these creatures are called *Reversible* Minkies is because, given any opportunity, they turn themselves inside out and display the behaviour you see now. When they do, there's really nothing for it but to wait patiently until they turn themselves back. So, will you all quietly reboot your Data-Globes and select your Mathematics modules."

With groans and glares at Boris, the class reluctantly pushed the large round buttons on the benches in front of them. Hazy orbs of colour floated in the air above each Poggle before clearing to reveal a 3D menu. One by one, they selected the word 'Mathematics' from the list and the colours were replaced by whirling shapes and numbers.

"Oh yes, before I go I need a volunteer to look after Spong outside of school hours." A sea of hands waved in front of Miss Lastic's nose, and there were cries of "Miss! Me! Pick me!" The teacher scanned the eager faces.

"Norman Snodgrass. I shall ask you to take care of him."

Norman jumped. He'd been so busy watching Spong, wondering what it meant if he turned green, that he hadn't even put up his hand.

"Th-Thank you, Miss Lastic," he stuttered, not quite sure what he was taking on.

Behind him, Boris Whinge hissed, "What does she want to give him to a long-toed freak like you for?"

"See me at the end of the day for some more care instructions, Norman," his teacher added. "Ah, here's Miss Take now."

Miss Take, the Maths teacher, entered through the sliding door and seemed to find it completely normal to see a Reversible Minky pinging off the classpod walls. She put on her Data-Helmet and adjusted the antennae. A few blue sparks whizzed above her head, then 3D images of triangles and pyramids were projected into the air.

Miss Take tried to conduct the lesson as usual but, to be honest, I'm not sure that any Poggle learned much about trigonometry that day. It's hard to focus on a Data-Globe when there's a Reversible Minky bouncing overhead.

A BRILLIANT INVENTION

'POFFFF!'

ANOTHER EXPLOSION FROM the nearby tube announced the arrival of Ernie Sludgebucket, a skinny Poggle with a slightly oversized hooter – Norman's best friend.

"How's it going, Norm?" Ernie asked brightly. "Found anything yet?"

"Hopeless," replied Norman. "Found one measly Double Bug, ended up with about a zillion and had to let 'em all go. You know what they're like…"

"Never mind; we've got twice the chance of finding something good now! Oooohhh…" He picked himself up from where the tube had dumped him and rubbed his rear. "These things are getting worse," he complained. "They either send you to the wrong place and suffocate you with dust, or fire you out like a cannonball. I don't know why the Elder Poggles don't fix them."

"That's what Mum said last night," agreed Norman, "but the Human who invented them has gone missing. Professor Zube his name is."

"You don't believe that, do you?" Ernie snorted. "My dad says the Elders spread a rumour about a mad Earth Human who landed here, created the Zubes then mysteriously disappeared. That way there's no one to blame for the mess they're in now. I mean, do you know anyone who has actually seen this professor?"

"No... now you mention it," said Norman thoughtfully, "I can't say I do."

With these thoughts hanging between them, the two companions resumed their search and, for a moment, the surface of the Planet was peaceful again.

Zube Tubes had sounded like a good idea at the time. The idea was simple enough and had struck the young Professor Zube in a moment of glorious inspiration forty years earlier...

Having recently landed on the Planet, he was sitting in a teapod, absent-mindedly observing the Poggle 'honking hour'. This involved crowds of Poggles queuing to squeeze through the maze of tunnels that snaked inside the Planet, as everyone tried to return to their home pods at the end of the day.

The trouble was, as hard as Poggles crammed themselves into one end of a tunnel, more Poggles were trying to squeeze into the opposite end. As a result, the normally mild-mannered creatures turned puce with rage and vented their frustration by honking their large, hooter-shaped noses – and so it became known as the 'honking hour'.

Professor Zube shook his head in amusement and sucked the last dregs of his mungoberry tea through a straw. Slowly, a smile crept over his face. Then, with a loud *"A-ha!"* that made his neighbour slop his drink, he began scribbling excitedly on his tea-stained napkin.

Six months later, the Green Planet had a shining system of plastic vacuum-tubing winding through it – rather like a vein of mould running through a nice piece of Gorgonzola cheese. Fortunately the tubes smelt far better, or no self-respecting Poggle would have gone anywhere near them.

Now all they had to do to travel was choose a destination from rows of tiny buttons at each tube entrance, step inside and wait. Within seconds, a door slid shut behind them and a whooshing vacuum sucked the Poggle through the tube. Along the way, mechanical flaps opened and closed with a swish, diverting the passenger to the chosen location. Just before arrival, the suction power eased off, allowing them to walk out normally.

The tubes were designed as a one-way system so there was no risk of colliding with a Poggle coming the other way, and the longest journey time from one side of the Planet to the other was now only ten seconds. Calm was restored and 'honking hour' was no more.

Sometimes inventions become so well known that they are named after their inventor. For instance, back on Earth in 1908, a man called Mr Hoover took two pillowcases, some piping and a bit of suction and found an interesting way of getting dust off his slippers. Nowadays nearly every home has one of these contraptions (much improved upon the original design) but rather than say, 'Could you pass me the two-pillow-pipe-sucker', we simply ask for the 'Hoover'. (Actually, my dad calls it the *'fluffy-up-the-tubey-hole'* – I think it could catch on.)

The same applied to the new travel tubes. The Professor actually called his invention a *'multi-dimensional-vacuum-powered-transportation-network'* but no Poggle could remember its name long enough to ask for directions to one, so they shortened it to 'Zube Tube'. Professor Zube was hailed as a hero and given the Freedom of the Planet.

That had been forty years ago, and for many years afterwards the Zube Tube network was a well-maintained, efficient form of transport, until one day... the Professor disappeared.

In his absence, the Zubes became very unreliable. Dust clogged the delicate mechanisms controlling suction and speed, and Poggles entering the network had no guarantee where they would end up. Popular destinations had piles of cushions at their exits to soften the falls of those being ejected at high speed. Sometimes the vacuum pressure dropped off altogether, leaving Poggles suspended in the tubes overhead.

The poor overworked TWITs spent all day running from one place to another...

Technically Worrying Incident Teams (TWITs for short) were set up to deal with the problem. The poor, overworked TWITs ran around all day with ladders and saws, cutting holes in the tubes and rescuing the stranded; they tried to seal the holes with rubber plant leaves, but none of this improved the performance of the network.

Once, the Zubes were shut down for a whole week when one TWIT used the wrong type of leaves. There was general pandemonium, and a petition was presented to the Elder Poggles at that week's assembly in the Star Chamber. As a result, Special Poggle Action teams for Network Needs and Emergency Repairs were created (SPANNERs for short). Things improved slightly but no one understood the system as well as Professor Zube.

There were rumours that he had gone to explore the Dark Side of the Planet but no one knew why, and now some people doubted that Professor Zube had ever existed.

LOST

ERNIE SLUDGEBUCKET WAS feeling pleased with himself.

He held his jar up to his snout and grinned at the contents crawling inside.

Two Humm Bugs, three Firelighters and, best of all, a Trojan! Miss Lastic will be chuffed! he thought. Trying not to seem too happy, he strolled over to his friend. "What have you got, then?" he asked casually.

"Nothing... zilch... diddly squat..." Norman replied. "I'm going to be in big trouble."

"It doesn't help that you're afraid to look anywhere in case a Scudder runs up your hooter," Ernie sympathised.

Just the mention of the word Scudder caused Norman to spin round nervously. His eyes darted from rock to rock, searching for a glimpse of a hairy black leg. Anyone who has a phobia of Earth spiders will understand the toe-curling feeling they gave him. Think of the most awful spider you can... now double the number of legs and imagine it running backwards, sideways and upside-down at lightning speed – and there you have a Scudder.

Norman sighed and shook his jar, hoping the grains of dust inside would spring into life… Nothing.

"Look, Norm, I've got more than enough bugs here – why don't you take the Firelighters?" Ernie pointed to three delicate, blue-winged flies circling in formation near the lid.

"Wow, thanks Ern, but how will we get them into my jar without them escaping?"

"Leave it to me," grinned Ernie taking a small bottle labelled 'SUGAR SYRUP' from his belt. He carefully unscrewed the lid of Norman's empty jar and dripped some of the sticky liquid into the bottom. "Right, hold it on its side," he instructed.

Norman did as he was told and Ernie slowly tipped his jar sideways so the necks met. He quickly whipped off his lid and closed the gap between the two. Instantly, the Firelighters picked up the scent of the syrup and darted into the empty container.

"Now!" shouted Ernie, and both Poggles clapped the lids back on their jars and tightened them.

"Ow!" Norman yelped, shaking first one hand then the other as he juggled the suddenly searing hot jar.

Inside, the Firelighters were doing their job, gorging on the sugar syrup and producing bright light and heat from their glowing bottoms. He put down the jar, and Spong ran around in circles, enjoying the warmth while the flies finished their meal.

"Useful little things," mused Ernie. "I wonder how the Elder Poggles managed before they discovered them? Dad said they had better eyesight in those days. I'd have been falling all over the place…" he tailed off nervously and gave Norman a sideways glance.

"Crikey," Norman laughed, "imagine what *I'd* have been like. I fall over in green daylight!"

Ernie was relieved to hear his friend make a joke, but in fact Norman wasn't like most Poggles. The middle toe on both of his feet was extraordinarily long and made him very clumsy. He normally fell over several times a day and, although most Poggles would politely pretend they hadn't noticed, Ernie often saw them staring. Worse still, some of their classmates, led by Boris Whinge and his gang, made a point of bullying Norman because he was different. To his credit, Ernie always stuck up for his friend even though this meant he was teased as well.

"Is that a Trojan you've got in there?" Norman asked, changing the subject.

"Yeah! I wonder what's inside it?" Ernie rattled his jar to encourage the Trojan to reveal its secret. It worked. The boring, brown beetle suddenly erupted into a frenzy of suckers and tentacles. It began climbing the side of the jar, leaving behind a slimy, fizzing trail of silver. At this, the nervous Humm Bugs began buzzing and vibrating their triangular, black and white striped bodies. This turned them grey so they blended into the background.

"That's upset them," laughed Norman.

"Could have been worse," said Ernie. "I once saw a Trojan with an acid dart that would have dissolved those Humm Bugs in seconds. Fantastic thing it was."

The warmth of the Firelighters finally faded, and the two Poggles picked up their things and headed back to the Zube Tube.

"I just would have liked to have found something really special," Norman said wistfully, prodding a small rock from the safe distance of his middle toe.

"What, you mean like a Baracs Beetle?!" replied Ernie. "That *would* be special."

"Yeah. Miss Lastic says poor old Fred is the last one on the Planet. Not much of a life for him, stuck in a tank in our classpod all day. To think there used to be thousands of them once… I wonder why they all died out."

"Hmm," pondered Ernie, "I guess *I'd* be feeling pretty sick if all I'd eaten for a hundred years was poo."

"Dung, you mean?" said Norman.

"Same thing. Mum says that's the reason we've got such a waste problem now – no Baracs Beetles to recycle it all like they used to."

"But doesn't it all just get sent to the Wasteland?" asked Norman.

"Yeah, but what do you think happens to it there?" replied Ernie.

"I don't know… I hadn't really thought about it." A puzzled look spread over Norman's face as he contemplated the problem.

It wasn't surprising that he hadn't thought about it. Poggles had developed a very neat way of dealing with their 'waste' which required very little concentration or effort. All Poggles wore a utility belt with a light that flashed every few days to remind them when it was time to be 'emptied'. This could be done by simply attaching a waste pipe to their star-shaped belly buttons and flipping another switch on their belt. A few seconds later, the light would go out and that was it. No mess, no fuss, no funny noises or smells and, best of all, no need to wash their hands afterwards.

The waste-pipe system was also created by Professor Zube. He designed it to run alongside the Zube Tube network so comfort was never far away. As the process only takes place every few days, a Poggle can quite easily be several inches thinner afterwards.

One TWIT thought that this would be a useful fact to help free a Poggle who had got stuck in a Zube. The poor thing's waste light had broken so he didn't realise he was well overdue for an emptying until he became firmly wedged on his morning commute to the Sugar Rock Mine. The poor Poggle obediently followed the TWIT's instructions and flipped his waste switch inside the Zube. In fairness, it did do the trick and un-bunged him, but it was a pretty unpleasant journey to work that day for all the Sugar Rock miners behind him!

Norman shook his head. It was no good; he had no idea what happened to his insides after they left his body and he didn't much care to think about it. He wiggled his toe absent-mindedly in the cool dust left by a recently shifted stone.

A tiny flash of white caught his eye. "Look! A Sneezewort!" he shrieked, pointing to an object exactly like a crumpled-up tissue on legs. Norman made a dive for the creature, catching his left toe in Spong's leash as he did so. There was a crash, a shattering of glass and three blue flies escaped into the late afternoon sky.

"Are you OK?" Ernie rushed to help his friend to his feet. "You've broken Miss Lastic's jar!"

"I know... My stupid toes! What am I going to do? I've let your Firelighters escape as well and... Oh no!"

The broken jar, escaped insects and fresh bruises were suddenly forgotten. Norman and Ernie watched in horror as an orange ball bounced away from them.

"Spong! NO!" they shouted.

Too late.

Trailing his leash wildly behind him, Spong reached the Zube Tube entrance. Delighted at finding himself free, he turned yellow and bounced up towards its shiny brass buttons. He hit one of them at random and rebounded into the tube. There was a *shush* as the doors closed and a *whoosh* as Spong disappeared from view.

Seconds later, Norman and Ernie reached the entrance just in time to see a light disappear behind a button with the word 'Wasteland' on it.

Trailing his leash wildly behind him...

THE FIB POT

ISADORA SNODGRASS WAS worried. As she stood washing the breakfast dishes, she knew, with a mother's instinct, that all was not well with her son.

Norman had been late home for supper the night before and had had a definite droop to his hooter. What's more, he'd hardly touched his food – splungewort mash on sugarloaf toast, his favourite.

When she'd asked him what was wrong, he'd mumbled something about not being able to do his homework and a broken jar. Well, the last part had been easily fixed. Isadora Snodgrass had a pantry full of clean jam jars waiting to be filled with her award-winning mungoberry preserve. She smiled for a moment and glanced at her collection of first-prize ribbons pinned above the sink. Then her frown returned as she plunged her hands once more into the foaming water and pulled out Norman's breakfast bowl. It reminded her – he'd not eaten his Wartflakes that morning either.

Norman's temperature had been normal; although, judging by the state of his bed, he'd clearly not slept well. Half of his sheets had been on the floor and the rest so tightly twisted around that it had taken an extra five minutes to get him out of bed. Isadora scrubbed vigorously at the bowl to remove a stubborn Wartflake.

Maybe he was just worried about Spong. He'd come home alone, saying Spong was a bit off colour so Miss Lastic had taken him to the vet. Yes, that must be it – he'd become very attached to the fluffy creature. With a satisfied nod, Isadora pulled the plug in the sink and watched the water drain away, first clockwise then anti-clockwise, down the plughole.

Of course, here on Earth, water quietly obeys the laws of physics and swirls in an orderly fashion one way or the other, depending on which hemisphere you are in. However, water on the Green Planet does pretty much what it wants. This is largely because the Planet doesn't spin on its axis as it moves around the Dog Star – but it's also just because it can. In fact, it's not uncommon for water to lurk in the sink long after you've pulled the plug, then whoosh away when you least expect it. The fact that the Planet moves in this fixed way also means that one side is in permanent daylight and the other in perpetual darkness; that side is known as the Dark Side and no Poggle ventures there.

Isadora picked up a worn tea towel, on which was a picture of a very old Poggle wearing a purple cloak and a gold pointed hat. She began drying the dishes as her husband Arthur strolled into the kitchen. He gave his wife an affectionate peck on the cheek.

"Lovely breakfast, Izzy."

Isadora smiled as her husband wound his arms around her, but said, "There's no time for that; I've these dishes to sort and then I'm off to the shops. We're out of teabags and I want to check the mungoberries at the market to see if they're ripe enough for my first batch of jam. Anything new in *The PUN*?"

"Just the usual, dear." Arthur unfolded his copy of *The Planet's Updated News* which had been tucked under his arm. "Waste levels have risen again… Slight upturn in the production of sugar; that'll please the boss… Oh, and a bit about the plans for Zohar's Golden Jubilee party."

Izzy held up her tea towel and stared at the kind old Poggle face in the picture. "I can't believe it's fifty years since he became Master Poggle! Where does time go?"

"You're not wrong, dear – I can hardly believe our Norman will be eight next birthday. Seems only yesterday that he was all legs and hooter and we were bringing him home from the maternity pod." Arthur Snodgrass smiled at the memory.

"That reminds me," his wife replied. "I'm worried about Norm. He's off his food."

Arthur Snodgrass did a double take. "Off his food? Norman? Are you sure?" he spluttered.

In life, there are those who eat to live and those who live to eat, and Norman fell very firmly, and slightly podgily, into the second camp.

"Certain. He's skipped two meals now."

"Two meals?!" Arthur blurted.

"Yes. Now, close your mouth and stop repeating everything I say. I think I know what's wrong with him." Isadora folded her tea towel purposefully. "He's fretting over Spong."

"Spo—" Arthur began, but checked himself quickly. "What do you mean, dear?" he managed instead.

"Well, he's obviously worried that Spong's been taken to the vet. You know how inseparable they've become."

She picked up a teapot and marched over to some shelves which were adorned with a variety of pots of different shapes, sizes and colours. Besides her prize-winning jam, Izzy Snodgrass's second passion was tea. She was famous for being able to brew exactly the right blend for every occasion, ailment or mood, and her advice was often sought on the subject.

"Oh, I meant to say, I'll be late home for supper tonight, dear. Bit of a rush on at the Sugar Rock Mine so I'm doing some overtime."

"Righto," replied his wife absent-mindedly. She reached up to put the teapot on the shelf next to a strange, cabbage-green pot whose spout appeared to be growing longer. Isadora drew her breath in sharply. "Arthur! Come and look at this! The Fib Pot's spout is growing!"

"The Fib Pot's spout is growing?" replied Arthur, unable to prevent himself from repeating her words. "What does that mean?"

"It means, dear husband, that someone in this family is telling lies…"

Someone in this family has been telling lies…

LIES

NORMAN FELT WRETCHED as he dawdled slowly into school. It had taken him ages to get to sleep, and when he'd finally drifted off he'd dreamt that Spong was floating in a jar full of giant bugs.

"Cheer up, Norm," Ernie said half-heartedly. "He's a friendly little thing. Someone's bound to be looking after him." It wasn't Ernie's most convincing performance and, in truth, he was just as worried.

"How am I going to face Miss Lastic?" Norm sighed. "No Spong and no homework! She'll kill me!"

"Just say the same thing that you said to your mum," Ernie replied.

"What, that Miss Lastic has taken him to the vet? She'll know *that's* not true!"

"No," explained Ernie patiently, "you tell Miss Lastic that your *parents* took Spong to the vet last night."

"Oh, I see," said Norm quietly, "I guess that would work. I'm a hopeless liar though – it makes me nervous."

"Look at it this way," suggested Ernie helpfully, "it's not *another* lie, it's the *same* lie told to a different person."

"I don't suppose I've got any choice," Norman replied dismally. "Mum's Fib Pot will be working overtime, though."

"One thing at a time, Norm. We'll deal with the Fib Pot later." Secretly, though, Ernie thought himself very lucky that his mum didn't own the awful thing.

The two Poggles walked on, heads down, scuffing the dirt. Ernie's jar of bugs swung gently from the hook on his belt, causing the insects inside to bump against the glass and buzz about. Norman's replacement jar hung empty, reminding him about the second problem on his mind. Of course, Ernie had offered him a Humm Bug but Norman didn't dare risk another catastrophe, and why should his friend lose out because of his own wretched clumsiness?

Normally the walk to school was enjoyable. Most young Poggles chose walking over Zube-ing to delay their arrival, and the two friends usually stopped to study the many strange plants that grew madly inside the Planet despite the lack of sunshine; it seemed that the warm light from the many jars of Firelighters was just as good.

A commotion broke out overhead as a rather overweight Poggle became stuck in a busy Zube Tube. One by one, more Poggles were ramming up behind him until finally, with a sound like a rubber bung being pulled out of a bottle, the jam freed itself and several Poggles cartwheeled out of sight to their respective destinations. This would usually have amused Norman and Ernie, but this morning, with their heads down, the two friends were oblivious.

Gradually, the path filled with other groups of Poggles all heading to the shiny white school pod in the distance. Norm spotted some of his classmates comparing jars of blurry objects with 'oohs' of amazement. His stomach turned again.

"Oi! Toe-freak! The idea is to put something *in* the jar before you bring it in!" The familiar, taunting sneer of Boris Whinge made Norman jump.

"Look, Jeli! He's found a jar of air! Now, that's what I call clever!" Boris grinned at a mean-faced Poggle beside him, who sneered back. Angelica Mould, or Jeli Mould as her friends called her, was never far from Boris's side and always ready to join in the taunting of his latest victim.

"I guess that's all we should expect of an airhead!" she smirked. The two of them laughed in Norman's face. Ernie silenced them.

"Well, it's obvious you idiots have never heard of Invisi-bugs."

Boris and Jeli stopped laughing and looked again at Norman's jar, not quite sure whether to believe him.

"Yeah, well, we've got to be going. Jeli's going to help me practise my hooting. I'm bound to be asked to do the solo at Zohar's party." And with that, the two unpleasant characters ran off, whispering to each other.

"They make me so mad!" Ernie fumed. "There's no way Whinger is going to get that solo before me. He's always off-key."

"Don't let him get to you, Ern," Norman tried to calm his friend. "You're much better than him and everyone knows it. Quick thinking about Invisi-bugs, too!"

"Thanks, but they'll know I was bluffing soon enough."

Their pace slowed as they reached the large oval doors of the school pod, which slid open to allow the stream of noisy

Poggles inside. Gradually the mob filtered off into the circular classpods dotted along the main corridor. Norman and Ernie ducked into the third one on the left, where the rest of Miss Lastic's form were busy seating themselves at their benches.

These were arranged in two circles. Twelve Poggles could fit around the outer circle and eight on the inner. An opening in each of the circles allowed the teacher through to a raised podium which contained various buttons and knobs.

There were some open cubbyholes near the door where a few of the crowd were busy storing their jam jars, bubble bags and lunch cubes. One set of cubbyholes, labelled 'Data-Helmets', was reserved for the teaching staff. Each of these contained a different metal hat with antennae sticking out of it.

Norman and Ernie squeezed into the inner circle and seated themselves on their stools furthest away from the door. A few moments later, their form teacher arrived and took her place in the middle.

The class stood and chanted, "Good *morning*, Miss *Lastic*."

"Good morning, class. Sit down, please. I hope you all managed to complete last night's homework? I'm looking forward to seeing what you have brought in."

Norman was convinced she looked straight at him, and he squirmed on his stool.

"Right, I'll take the register; and when I call your name, please bring your jars up so we can all see them."

Miss Lastic pushed a button on her central panel and a list of names was projected onto the wall. One by one, Norman's classmates left their seats and marched proudly into the middle of the classpod.

"Anna Conda… Oh, well done, Anna! Two Firelighters and a nice big Scudder!"

Norman's day was getting worse by the minute. He shuffled to the farthest edge of his stool, away from where Anna was waving her jar excitedly for all to see.

"Theresa Green… Not bad at all, Theresa; a Spring Fly and a Marge Fly. Now, class, you see the back legs on this Spring Fly? These are tightly coiled and enable it to launch itself into flight with alarming speed. No, Theresa… we don't want to see your impression of a Spring Fly."

"Miss, why is a Marge Fly called a Marge Fly?" Anna Conda asked as she peered into her neighbour's jar.

"Well, because they are just like the Butterflies found on Earth – only less fat."

Norman was usually fascinated to hear Miss Lastic explain about the various insects (except Scudders, of course), but as each Poggle collected their jar he could only think of his approaching turn. This was one occasion when he was glad his surname was near the end of the alphabet.

"Angelica Mould… Hmm, another Firelighter, but… have you pulled its legs off?!" Miss Lastic studied the poor creature, which had no choice but to flutter endlessly around the jar, having no legs to land on.

"No, Miss! Of course not!" Jeli protested indignantly.

"Then why is there something that looks suspiciously like a leg stuck to your finger?"

Miss Lastic fixed Jeli with one of her stares, which were far worse than any words that ever came from her mouth. Jeli went scarlet and quickly returned to her seat.

"Angelica Mould…
have you pulled its legs off?"

"Ernie Sludgebucket… Good effort, Ernie! Two Humm Bugs and a Trojan. Do you know what this one does?"

"Suckers, tentacles and fizzy slime!" Ernie replied excitedly.

"Ah, *Trojanus Octopussus Fizzicalis*! Very nice."

Ernie returned to his seat with a big grin on his face and, despite his fate, Norm managed to smile back.

"Norman Snodgrass."

The smile vanished. It seemed to take an age for him to walk to the shelves of jars, select his empty one and shuffle up to the central console.

"What's this, Norman?" Miss Lastic's penetrating gaze fixed upon him.

"Nothing, Miss," mumbled Norman.

"I can see that perfectly well. Explain."

Norman gulped and looked at his friend for some last-minute, desperate help. Behind Ernie, Boris Whinge's spotty face erupted into a grin.

"Spong!" mouthed Ernie. Of course.

"I'm-afraid-I-didn't-have-time-to-do-the-homework-last-night-Miss-Lastic-I-had-to-go-with-my-parents-to-take-Spong-to-the-vet-he's-not-well," Norman garbled without breathing. He really was a terrible liar.

Miss Lastic studied Norman's face intently, her shrewd eyes locking onto his.

At last she said, "Very well, I'll give you until the end of the week to come up with something, but no excuses then."

A sharp exhalation from his left told him that Ernie hadn't been breathing either. "Well done!" Ernie whispered as Norm returned thankfully to his place. Norman didn't feel as if he'd done anything to be proud of at all.

"Aw, is poor iddle Spongy-Wongy sick, then? Sick of being with a creep like you, more like!" Boris leaned forward and sneered quietly.

"Boris Whinge." Miss Lastic's voice made him jump.

"Wh-what, Miss?" he stuttered.

"Your homework, of course, Boris."

The class giggled as Boris sloped over to the last remaining jar in the cubbyholes.

"Very nice, Boris; a Sneezewort." The smug grin returned. "Now, you have to be careful with Sneezeworts, or *Kleenexus Snotificus* to give them their proper name. They live by disguising themselves as tissues and waiting for someone to sneeze and mistake them for a hanky. Then they feed off the… Yes, well, it's all pretty unpleasant. The trouble is they harbour germs and can pass on all sorts of bugs. I hope you washed your hands after you collected this one, Boris?"

Boris shifted guiltily and tried to hide his grimy fingers that hadn't seen clean water for a very long time.

"Now, class, we will keep these insects for two weeks to enable us to care for them and study them, then we will release them again. Please return your jars to the shelves and line up for assembly."

There was a scraping of stools and a clatter of three-toed feet as twenty Poggles all tried to head for the door at once.

"Two lines, and don't run! How many times must I tell you?" Miss Lastic chided wearily.

SPIES

THE WEEKLY ASSEMBLY in the Star Chamber was not like the dull assemblies held in Earth schools. For a start, everyone on the Planet attended, so it was a huge gathering. Important news was shared, decisions were made, and occasionally punishments were dealt out to those who had disobeyed the Poggle Charter.

This didn't happen often as, by and large, Poggles were a peaceful, law-abiding bunch. Not surprisingly, the role of Poggle Warden – a bit like our policemen – was not a challenging one. As a result, one or two Wardens created petty rules to increase their own importance, but this was usually stamped out by the Elder Poggles.

The central Star Chamber in the heart of the Green Planet was an impressive space. Naturally circular, as most rooms on the planet were, its roof was alight with a hundred glass globes. These were filled with Firelighters, gorging on sugar and emitting their bright radiance and heat. It was a full-time job for an old Poggle called Flint Zippo to ensure the lanterns never went out. The job had been passed down through the Zippo family for generations and they carried out their duty with pride.

As Norman filed into the chamber with his class, he was once again struck by the majestic surroundings and seriousness of the occasion. There was no question of misbehaving in here. Even Boris Whinge looked as if butter wouldn't melt in his mouth as he took his seat on a semi-circular bench near the front of the room. Ernie was sitting beside him, not through choice but because this bench was reserved for the Hooting Choir and both were members.

Above their heads in the viewing galleries, the adult Poggles arrived through the many Zube Tube outlets, fitted with special, star-shaped openings. Norman could just make out his parents seated above and to his right. Mum wore her best feathered hat as usual, and Dad his smartest trilby.

Once everyone was gathered, a signal was given. The Hooting Choir stood and raised their trumpet-shaped snouts to the roof. The crowd fell silent as the melodious sound of the Green Planet Anthem drifted around them. Poggle hooting is a bewitching cross between bagpipes and humming, the sound of which has been known to send some into an almost trancelike state.

As the music reached its climax, the heavy purple curtains at the front of the chamber drew back silently. Now the whole assembly stood as six Elder Poggles processed in and waited behind some small wooden stools on the raised platform. A seventh stool was left unoccupied in the centre and, as the last chord of the anthem echoed around the room, Zohar, Master Poggle, entered the chamber. His purple robe flowed behind him and his gold hat shone in the firelight. The hem of his robe was decorated alternately with small silver bells and embroidered mungoberries. The silver bells tinkled as he walked.

"Greetings, fellow Poggles, and be seated," came the usual salute.

There was a shuffling of stools and benches as the throng of Poggles settled down attentively. Norman loved assemblies. Although he tried to pay attention to what was going on, the Master Poggle's gentle, lilting voice usually sent him into a happy daydream, far from Boris Whinge's cruel taunts. For the first time since losing Spong, his stomach unknotted slightly.

"Greetings, fellow Poggles, and be seated."

"I'm pleased to tell you," Zohar began, "that the production of sugar has increased this week. I'm sure we would all like to thank the members of the mining team who have worked so hard to achieve this."

An appreciative ripple of applause ran around the room. The core of the Green Planet was made of pure sugar which was a staple Poggle food.

"Unfortunately, our waste levels are still rising." Murmurs of concern could now be heard. "We will continue to monitor the Waste Dome, and we have an expert working to find a long-term solution to the problem…"

After what seemed to Norman like a few moments, but was actually half an hour, Miss Lastic ushered her class out of the chamber and back to the nearby school pod. Ernie caught up with his friend along the way.

"Nice hooting, Ern," said Norm.

"Glad you think so," grinned his mate. "Hard to hear with Whinger rasping away in my ear, though."

The rest of the day passed uneventfully. Their first lesson was Geography with Mrs Sippy – a middle-aged Poggle with a twinkle in her eye whose favourite subject was Earth. She claimed to have been part of a Poggle Exploration Team (PET) sent to Earth to look for intelligent life, and she made a point of dropping this fact into every lesson. You could say it was her PET subject.

There had been great excitement on the Green Planet when, forty years earlier, the first PET landed in a cornfield in a place called Wiltshire, in the United Kingdom. However, after months of studies and seeing the mess the Humans were making of their home, the PET reached the conclusion that perhaps they weren't so intelligent after all, and the search continued. There was one exception – a young Professor who had begged to be allowed to return with them.

Geography was nearly over, and Mrs Sippy was indulging herself again.

"Oh, we used to have such fun," she began. "Every time we landed in a field on Earth the Humans would go mad about the patterns our spaceship left behind! So then, every PET would make a point of stopping there whenever they passed nearby, to leave fresh marks. You should have seen them waving their arms in excitement," she giggled, "and then we'd tune into their radio stations on the way home to listen to the nonsense they came out with. All over a pile of smashed grass!"

She wiped her eyes as the buzzer went for the end of the lesson. The many classpod doors flew open and streams of Poggles ran into the spacious playpod at the end of the main corridor.

Norm and Ernie picked their way through the crowd. Some were playing Spaceball, trying to keep an almost weightless, jelly-like ball in the air using only the power of thought. You had to position yourself underneath it and skilfully will the ball up into the cup-shaped helmet on your head. All the while, the opposing team tried to jostle you out of the way. Once you had the ball, you had to run the length of the pitch and flick it into your opponent's goal. Points were deducted if you were the last person to touch the ball before it hit the ground.

Norm was hopeless at Spaceball, or any activity that required balance, because of his long toes. He usually sat at the side of the playpod, looking on with Ernie.

"Right," began Ernie when they had found a bench out of earshot, "we need a plan."

"A plan for what?" Norm felt uneasy.

"To get Spong back, of course! We have to go to the Wasteland!" Ern waved his hands excitedly.

"B-but, we can't… I mean, how do we know he'll still be there? He could have bounced anywhere by now!"

Ernie hadn't thought of that. He paused, frowned and said "Well, we have to start somewhere. Maybe he'll have left some tracks behind."

Norm couldn't think of any more arguments, and by the time break had finished he'd reluctantly agreed to sneak out of his pod and meet Ern half an hour after bedtime. They would then take the nearest Zube Tube to the Wasteland.

As they left their bench to head for the next class – Poggish with Miss Interpret – they failed to spot a shadowy figure hiding in the bushes nearby. Boris Whinge emerged from the undergrowth. He'd been searching for a stray Spaceball and was delighted to find himself eavesdropping on their plan.

We'll see about that, he thought to himself.

"They failed to spot a shadowy figure hiding in the bushes nearby."

As the day wore on, Norman became more and more convinced that the plan was a foolish one and doomed to fail. There was no chance to persuade Ernie to call it off, though – he had hooting practice after school – so Norman walked home alone.

What a mess, he thought; *why didn't I just come clean to Mum and Dad in the first place?*

The simplicity of this idea suddenly struck him. What an idiot he was. Spong was missing, he'd lied to his parents and his teacher, he still had to do yesterday's homework and, worst of all, he'd agreed to go to the Wasteland tonight. He wouldn't be surprised if the Fib Pot's spout met him halfway home. It was bound to be miles long by now. Yes – he was a complete idiot.

Supper was an awkward one. Isadora Snodgrass made tea in the Fib Pot, and its oversized spout slopped liquid everywhere as she poured. No one spoke. Norman felt as though he would explode if this went on much longer and, try as he might, he couldn't stop the end of his hooter from trembling.

Arthur Snodgrass was also in some discomfort. He stole a sideways glance at his son. The poor Poggle looked wretched. Isadora tried to pour a third cup of tea but the spout drenched a plate of Green Bug butter sandwiches and something inside Norm snapped.

"Mum, I…" he began.

"Izzy, there's something I need to tell you," his father interrupted, flashing Norman a meaningful look.

Isadora Snodgrass put the Fib Pot down.

"What is it, dear?" she said quietly.

"It's my fault the Fib Pot is like that... I haven't been entirely honest with you."

"Go on..."

"Well, when I said I had to work late tonight, it wasn't completely true. I was round at Bill Sludgebucket's trying out his home-brewed Pogginton Beer. I'm very sorry."

For a moment Isadora said nothing and just watched the Fib Pot. Gradually its spout shivered and began to shrink.

"You of all people should know better, Arthur," she said finally, and there was the faintest glimmer of a smile at the corner of her mouth. "I'll fetch a cloth." She bustled into the kitchen.

Arthur Snodgrass looked at the pot, whose spout had stopped shrinking but was still much longer than normal. He looked at his son... then, with a wink, popped a tea cosy over the green monstrosity.

"I trust you to do the right thing," was all he said.

TO THE WASTELAND

NORMAN'S HEART WAS pounding. He was certain his parents would hear and come to see what the noise was. He'd gone to bed twenty-five minutes earlier and had pretended to be asleep when his mum checked to make sure he wasn't reading under the covers. Nothing could be further from the truth.

In five minutes' time, he'd agreed (who knew why) to meet Ernie and go on a crazy search for Spong. At this present moment he doubted he would have the courage to get out of bed, let alone make it all the way to the Wasteland.

FOUR MINUTES.

Norm wiggled his toes and persuaded one foot to let itself be dangled out of bed. So far, so good. The other foot seemed happy enough to follow and soon both feet were on the floor, but his body was reluctant to leave the warmth of its fleecy blanket.

All I've got to do is straighten my legs and I'll be standing, he thought to himself, but his knees wobbled uncooperatively.

He gave them a stiff talking to and they stiffened up. He was standing.

THREE MINUTES.

Feeling a little braver now that he had achieved the impossible, he quickly stuffed a pillow under his blanket in case Mum should look in again on her way to bed. She'd be worried if she didn't see a Norm-shaped lump under the cover. Norman glanced down at his flabby blue stomach bulging over his utility belt and stuffed a second pillow into the bed for good measure. That should do it.

TWO MINUTES.

The squeak of his bedpod door made him freeze in the hall. Luckily, his parents were watching a comedy programme on the Telescreen and burst into hoots of laughter at the same moment. They were still chuckling as a small shadow sneaked down the hallway to the front door.

ONE MINUTE.

Norm fumbled with the latch, and it clattered as if a mob of the worst burglars on the Planet were trying to break in. Norm glanced fearfully behind him. Suddenly, his dad strode out of the living pod still talking to his mum over his shoulder. He headed in the opposite direction towards the kitchen, totally unaware of his son silhouetted against the front door behind him.

Norm had to act fast before his father returned. With a last fumble he loosened the catch and opened the front door just wide enough to squeeze through (which was pretty wide in Norm's case). Without looking back, he quickly pulled it to and headed down his garden path to the gate.

Little did he know that someone had watched him leave. Underneath his bed, eight glittering eyes sparkled in the dark. They belonged to a Scudder.

I wonder where he's off to…? Scheherazade (for that was the Scudder's name) thought to herself. *It's most unlike him.*

"*Little did he know that someone had watched him leave…*"

Of course, Norman would have been horrified to learn that a Scudder lived under his bed, but in fact Scheherazade (known as Sherri to her friends) had been there since the day he was born. It didn't matter to her that he hated Scudders – a fact she had discovered when she crawled onto the bed to see the new baby. She soon disappeared when Norm started screaming!

Now, Sherri only crept out when she was sure Norman was asleep. Then she would climb up the bedcovers and sit on his pillow to watch over him and whisper stories in his ear – she was an excellent storyteller. This was probably because she was named after a famous lady on Earth who told a thousand and one tales to the King of Persia to save her life. He was so enchanted by these adventures that he made her his Queen. Sherri loved the fact that they shared the same name.

"You're late!" A hiss from the bushes made Norm leap from his skin. Ern scrambled out of the hedge.

"You're lucky I'm here at all," whispered Norm. "I can't believe I let you persuade me this was a good idea."

"Well, you're here now so we might as well get on with it. Things can't get any worse." Ern sounded unusually gloomy.

"What's up?"

"Boris Whinge, that's what's up. I was in the middle of my audition for the hooting solo – you know, the high bit where you really have to breathe hard – and the creep stuck a drawing pin in my backside. I went all off-key and screechy."

"That's outrageous!" shouted Norm, forgetting for a moment that they were on a secret mission. "What did Miss Harmony say?"

"Well, I tried to explain, but I was so angry; I kept breathing in all the wrong places after that so she's gone and given the solo to *him*!"

The sight of his friend looking so utterly dejected spurred Norman into action.

"Right, come on," he said. "We're off to the Wasteland. Once we've found Spong, we can sort Whinger out once and for all. He's gone too far this time."

Norm strode off into the night, muttering to himself. Ernie hurried behind, feeling excited once more about their adventure.

They very nearly didn't make it to the end of the road. In his angry state, Norm didn't spot the glow of a Firelamp rounding the corner. Only Ernie's quick reaction, pulling him into another hedge, prevented him from running straight into Bert Snatchitt, their local Poggle Warden.

Bert wasn't someone you wanted to meet at any time. Not in the daytime when you were minding your own business, and certainly not when you were sneaking around after bedtime. He gave Poggle Wardens a bad name and was always on the lookout for someone to intimidate and threaten. Norm stifled a squeak.

"Right then, where are you…? Thirty minutes after bedtime, young Master Whinge said, so you ought to be here by now. Up to no good he said, and I won't have that… not on my watch," Bert muttered to himself; and he swung his lamp into the bushes, missing the end of Ern's snout by millimetres. Ernie felt the heat building up on the end of his hooter – he would have to move…

Suddenly there was a whistling noise. Bert jerked round to see Flint Zippo on his way home from tending the Firelighters in the Star Chamber.

"Evening, Bert, what are you up to?" Flint asked with a gleam in his eye.

"Acting on a tip-off if you must know," replied Bert, drawing himself up to his full height. "I'm reliably informed that those two mischief-makers, Snodgrass and Sludgebucket, are planning a moonlit flit around about now. I'm going to catch them at it."

"Norman and Ernie, you mean? Mischief-makers? I think someone's pulling your leg, Bert – why, you couldn't meet two nicer young Poggles. Who's your informant?"

"No, no, it wouldn't be right for me to divulge my sources," said Bert pompously. "The Poggle Public have to know they can approach me in total confidence with this sort of information."

"Quite," said Flint, trying to stop the corners of his mouth from turning up, "but if it was that Boris Whinge I'd take it with a pinch of salt. Everyone knows he has a grudge against those two. He's most likely sent you on a wild Scudder chase over here to throw you off the scent of something he's up to himself."

Bert Snatchitt turned red but quietly said, "Like I say, I can't divulge – but I'm confident I'm acting on sound information."

"Well, it's good to know you're on the case, Bert. The streets wouldn't be safe without you!" And openly chuckling to himself, Flint Zippo strolled off.

Bert waited until he was out of earshot then blurted, "That bloomin' Boris Whinge! Of course it's a cover-up. He must think I arrived on the Planet yesterday!" With a furious snort, Bert turned on his heel and headed off in the direction of Boris's home pod.

Silence fell again, only to be broken by the rustling of bushes as Norm and Ernie stumbled out. Ernie rubbed his overheated hooter.

"I don't believe it!" exclaimed Norm.

"He must have overheard us in the playpod!" muttered Ernie. "He's really done it this time!"

"Well, Boris will get a shock when Snatchitt turns up at his door, and it serves him right. Now, let's get out of here before anything else happens." Norman led the way again.

The two Poggles ran around the corner and along the path, keeping to the shadows. Soon they spotted the familiar sight of a luminous glass globe painted with a large capital Z, marking the entrance to their nearest Zube Tube. They entered and Ernie positioned his middle finger over the button marked 'Wasteland'. The friends exchanged nervous glances and Ernie pushed it.

There was a *shush* and a *whoosh* and ten seconds later the intrepid adventurers stepped out into the dingy green gloom. The smell of rotten eggs hung in the air, and an occasional 'blooping' noise could be heard as bubbles of gas broke the surface of the many mud pools that surrounded them.

"Blibey, whad a disgustig place!" said Norm, holding his hooter.

"Yeah, we should have come here to do our homework – it's crawling with bugs!" Ern swatted at a Spring Fly that had just landed on his ear.

Norm eyed the ground, nervously looking for Scudders, and frowned.

"What are they doing? They're all heading in the same direction over that hill."

He pointed towards a small mound in the distance, above which the air was black with flies.

"Better have a look… No sign of Spong here, anyway."

Ernie moved off and Norm followed, treading carefully and flinching at every scuttling insect in his path.

A few moments later they scrambled up to the top of the hill. An incredible stench hit their nostrils, making their eyes water. They rubbed their faces and, as the tears cleared, gasped at what they saw.

"They gasped at what they saw…"

Spread beneath them was a huge polythene dome, which rippled and pulsed as if it were alive. Hundreds of dirty, brown waste pipes rose from the ground surrounding it, feeding filth into the already straining structure. At the edges of the dome, bubbles of gas escaped with loud 'bloops' and trickles of waste seeped out, attracting clouds of flies. The whole thing looked like it would explode at any minute.

"What on the Planet is that?" exclaimed Norm.

"It must be the Waste Dome," replied Ern. "Zohar keeps talking about it in assembly… I never imagined it would be as revolting as this."

"Surely Spong wouldn't be here?" Norm gazed at the eyesore in front of him and tried to imagine what a curious furry creature would do in this place. He studied the ground again for any signs of bounce marks in the dust. "There's no sign of him, Ern; we ought to go back."

Norm turned round to his friend – but he was gone.

"Ern? Ernie! Where are you? Don't mess about!"

SILENCE.

"Ern, I'm not kidding – this is no time to play games!" Norm looked back down the hillside. He could just make out the entrance to the Zube Tube through the smog. Nothing. "Ern, I'm really sc—"

"Wow! You'll never guess what I've found!" Ernie's grinning face popped up from a nearby crater.

"Don't ever do that again! I thought the Scudders had got you. Have you found Spong?"

"Sorry, mate, I slipped into this hole and… it's amazing – come and see!" He disappeared again, leaving Norm no choice but to follow or be left alone.

Norm descended into the hole. It opened out into a large cave-like space. As his eyes adjusted to the dim light, he made out the shape of Ernie further in, beckoning him over. He followed and saw a huge pair of double wooden doors set into the far wall of the cave. One was slightly ajar, giving out a shaft of warm light.

"Whaddya make of this, then?" whispered Ernie excitedly.

"Wow! I've never seen doors like that before. They look so old. Who on the Planet needs something that big?" Secretly Norm didn't really want to know.

"We could always go in and find out?" Ern took a step towards the open door.

"You have *got* to be kidding!" hissed Norm. "We should get out of here!"

"Shh! Listen!" Ernie cocked his ear to the door. A faint squeaking came from inside.

"It can't be!" Norm shook his head in disbelief. "Spong!" he shouted.

The squeaks increased in volume and, without thinking, Norm pushed open the door and hurried in.

He found himself in a vast hallway. The floor was highly polished and made of small sections of wood, glued down in a neat pattern. (On Earth we would call this a parquet floor but Norman had never seen anything like it.) Halfway down the hall was a high side-table, over which hung an arched mirror. Loosely tied to one of the table legs was a leash, which led to a sumptuous, red velvet cushion on the floor below. In the middle of the cushion, a furry orange creature was squeaking and wriggling excitedly.

"Spong!" cried Norman and Ernie as they ran towards him.

Norman scooped him up, and Ernie ruffled his fur happily. Spong turned a golden yellow and burst into contented purrs and trills.

"Where have you been, you naughty Minky? You shouldn't have bounced off. I've been so worried about you!" Norm tried to scold his companion but couldn't hide his joy on being reunited. "Come on, we'd better get you home." He reached to untie the leash from the table leg.

"Look at this," said Ernie, standing on tiptoe and squinting at a jar of brown liquid resting on top of the table. A neat label on the jar said 'Sample No. 263', with that day's date below it. "Funny thing to have in a place like this… I wonder what it is?" He reached for the jar.

"DON'T TOUCH THAT!" boomed a voice behind them.

THE LABORATORY

NORMAN AND ERNIE were glued to the spot. Reflected behind them, in the mirror above the hall table, they saw a giant. Or rather, they could see the arms and legs of an enormous creature covered in strange grey material – its head was out of view.

"Sorry, I really didn't mean to shout," the creature spoke again. "It's just that the jar is contaminated. I never touch them without my gloves, and I didn't want you to pick up something nasty."

None of this made any sense to the two terrified Poggles, who remained motionless. Spong, on the other hand, was still squeaking happily and straining on his leash towards the giant.

"Ah, Spong! Didn't I tell you they'd come looking for you? I take it from your excitement that I have the honour of meeting Norman Snodgrass and Ernie Sludgebucket! What an absolute pleasure. I'm Professor Zube."

Norman and Ernie watched the reflections of their eyes widen and their mouths drop open. Slowly they turned and saw… not a scary giant but their first ever Human Being. True, he was about three feet taller than them and wore peculiar clothes (a grey suit) with round objects on it (buttons), but his face, although stranger than anything they had ever seen, was smiling and looked friendly enough. His skin was much paler than theirs (and not blue, of course) and the top of his head was shiny, with tufts of white hair.

"Reflected behind them…
they saw a giant…"

He wore two small rounds of glass in front of his eyes, which were held there by some gold wire tucked behind his ears. Most peculiar.

"Oh dear, this must all be very alarming for you. Never seen a Human Being before, of course. Well, while you come to terms with it, why don't you come through to my Laboratory and I'll rustle us up a snack. You must be hungry – it's nearly midnight."

The mention of food brought Norman partially to his senses and he managed a nod. Professor Zube moved off down the corridor and Spong ran happily after him, the taut lead jerking Norman into motion. He and Ernie followed stiffly, their eyes darting wildly to take in the strange sights around them. They passed several dark doorways until they reached another huge pair of wooden doors, carved with a detailed arrangement of cogs and dials.

Professor Zube stopped in front of them, reached forward and turned the large central dial left and right in a series of quick turns. In a few moments the entire doorway became a mass of movement as the seemingly ornamental, carved cogs began to whir and click into life. Slowly the great portal creaked and parted inwards.

Norman and Ernie had no idea what to expect next but felt disappointed when the doors opened to reveal nothing but a small, white, cube-shaped room. It was completely empty except for two large buttons on the far wall – one red and one green.

"Airlock," explained Professor Zube simply, stepping forward into the room. "Can't be too careful. Come on in."

Norm and Ern stepped inside mechanically, still unable to speak. Professor Zube pressed the red button and the wooden doors creaked shut behind them with a hollow thud. The green button lit up and the Professor pushed it firmly.

"Welcome to my Laboratory."

Slowly and silently, the entire end wall of the cube room slid sideways to reveal a sight that finally loosened the Poggles' tongues.

"Wow!" gasped Ernie.

"That's incredible!" whispered Norm.

In front of them, a rainbow of coloured jars, bottles, flasks, beakers, pipes and bowls was arranged on row upon row of shelves that lined the room. There were many wooden benches, upon which different-coloured liquids and solutions bubbled, steamed and hissed in their containers.

Their eyes absorbed the mix of jewelled colours reflecting the light from the bright white airlock. There were piles of bound paper stacked around the floor (they would later learn that these were books). Some lay open and revealed pages of spidery writing and diagrams. A mixture of smells assailed their hooters, some pleasant and citrusy, others faint and musky. Occasionally they caught a whiff that reminded them of the stench of the Waste Dome, which must be somewhere above their heads.

"Look!" said Norm, pointing to a square glass chamber, inside which was a perfect miniature of the Dome, complete with oozing waste and glooping gas bubbles.

"Ah, you've spotted my working model!" Professor Zube almost skipped across the room. He placed his hands into two rubber sleeves with gloves on the end that were set into the side of the glass. He twiddled absent-mindedly with some of the dials inside the chamber and the miniature Dome quivered slightly, emitting gloops of gas at a faster rate. Professor Zube frowned.

"Is everything alright?" asked Ernie.

"Hmm? Oh yes, of course, nothing for you to worry about… I mean, nothing to worry about at all. Just an experiment I'm doing to pass the time – no reason…" he tailed off unconvincingly. "Anyway, where are my manners? I promised you something to eat."

A few moments later, three comfy armchairs and side tables had been rescued from beneath piles of books and papers, and an array of strange yet tempting food was spread out. Norm, never one to be afraid to try new delights, spluttered in between mouthfuls.

"Lovely sandwiches; what's inside them?"

"Cheese and cucumber, and egg and cress. Glad you like them."

"Cheezenqcumber – how strange – and what does an Eggencress look like?" Norm asked politely between mouthfuls.

Meanwhile, Ernie was grappling with some small brown cylinders impaled on tiny sticks.

"Those are cocktail sausages," explained Professor Zube; "you don't—"

"OW!" squealed Ernie, clamping his mouth around the sausage, stick and all.

"… eat the sticks," finished Professor Zube.

Apart from this incident, their midnight feast was very pleasant. The two Poggles soon forgot that it was anything other than ordinary to be awake at this hour, far from their beds and eating strange-sounding food with a Human Being. While they ate, Professor Zube described his arrival on the

Planet (the two Poggles were amazed to learn that Mrs Sippy's PET tales were true) and his invention of the Zube Tube.

"But why did you disappear, Professor, and why have you let the Zubes get into such a state?" asked Norman.

"Yes, I suppose I ought to give you an explanation," the Professor replied seriously. "Pass me that small globe from the table over there, would you?"

Norm walked over to a nearby table stacked with labelled jars similar to the one they had seen earlier. In front of these was a green glass globe which shone brightly on one side and yet was dark on the other. It seemed to be almost full of a brown sludgy substance. He took a step forward to pick up the globe, not spotting a pile of books in his path. Norm lurched forward, crashing into the side of the table, and slid into a heap on the floor.

In painful slow motion, the globe rolled slowly towards the edge of the table. Norm was rolling too, trying to get up but hampered by his round belly. The globe reached the edge of the table and gently tipped over. With a soft 'smat', it plopped safely onto Norm's stomach, coming to rest in his belly button.

CRASH!

A glass jar on the other side of the table didn't have the same fortunate landing and now lay in pieces on the floor. Its stinking contents oozed towards a pile of books.

"GREAT HEAVENS!" shouted Professor Zube.

"I'm so sorry, Professor. I'll clean it up and bring you a new jar..." Norm stood up miserably, still holding the green globe. He offered it to the Professor who, to his surprise, wore a beaming smile.

"The timing – it's perfect! I should have realised... Oh, how wonderful... Wait till I tell Zohar..." he chattered excitedly.

Norm exchanged puzzled glances with Ernie, who shrugged his shoulders.

"Professor, what are you talking about?" Ernie asked.

"Oh, my dear Poggle, do you realise what Norm is?" The Professor was almost laughing now.

"Er... clumsy?" suggested Ern with an apologetic glance at his friend.

"No, no, no," giggled the Professor, taking Norm by both shoulders and crouching to stare directly into his eyes. "You, my dear, dear Poggle, are a Long... Toed... Poggle!" He clapped his hands with glee.

"Yes, I know I have long toes... They're a complete nuisance. That's why I always fall over. It's as if I feel the ground moving, and over I go. I'm so sorry about the jar." Norman was confused.

"Oh, bother the marvellous jar. I don't mind if you break all the jars in the place. Of course you fall over, it's what you were designed to do, my Long-Toed friend! You are a miracle! One of the last of your kind... Never thought I'd see the like again. Come, come, sit, sit."

The two Poggles sat down again in utter bewilderment.

"My poor Poggle," Professor Zube chuckled, "I don't doubt that all your life you have felt like some sort of misfit, not quite the same as all the rest. Hmm?"

Norman felt unwilling tears prick his eyes at this painfully accurate summary of himself.

"Well, the truth is, you are very special indeed, but many years ago Long-Toed Poggles were common. It would have been unusual to find the Short-Toed ones that live on the Planet today." Norm and Ernie listened in amazement.

"Yes, you are all descended from the original Long-Toed population who, far from being ridiculed for their supposed clumsiness, were recognised for their useful skills. You say you feel as if the ground moves, Norman, yet no one else seems to notice?"

Norm nodded vigorously.

"Well, that's exactly what happens. Your extra-long toes give you the ability to pick up the slightest vibration on the Planet's surface. If tuned correctly, you would be able to tell if danger were approaching and warn others. Your ancestors were masters of this art; and what you now feel is an embarrassment, is in fact a very great gift."

"But how come I'm the only one left?" Norm's voice cracked with the strange mix of emotions he was suddenly feeling.

"Oh, occasionally the trait reappears in individuals but they usually try and hide it. There are not many alive now who understand its significance. Of course, most of the original Long-Toed Poggles were killed in the Great War."

"What Great War?" Ern asked innocently.

"Good heavens, what do they teach you in school?" exclaimed the Professor. "Next you'll be telling me you haven't heard of the Drones!"

At the mention of the word, Norm and Ernie suddenly felt very cold and neither wanted to ask the question. Beside them on the floor, Spong whimpered and turned blue.

"Great Scott! You *don't* know what they are, do you? Well, I am deeply sorry to have to enlighten to you." The Professor suddenly looked incredibly sad.

"Many years ago, long before you were born and long before I came here, the Green Planet was attacked by the most awful creatures you can imagine. They came from their own Dark Planet and took over the Dark Side of this Planet. In the Great War that followed, the Long-Toed Poggles fought bravely. They were able to sense when the Drones were approaching and set traps for many of them. For a short time it even looked as though they might win, until one day the Drones found the only weakness the Long-Toed Poggles possessed."

"What was it?" blurted Norman.

The Professor made no reply but turned to a short-stemmed glass on the table beside him. Silently he licked his finger and began to run it around the rim of the glass. A sweet, pure note reverberated from it, which made Norm's toes tingle pleasantly. The Professor stopped and opened a small leather case that sat on the table beside the glass. Inside this were a number of two-pronged metal forks. The Professor selected one of the forks and struck it violently on the table. The Poggles jumped as a searing note of the same pitch rang out from the fork. Norm's toes were now aching.

Quickly, the Professor touched the fork to the rim of the glass. For a moment the sound magnified as the glass and fork vibrated in harmony, then there was a splintering noise and silence. The glass had shattered.

"Blimey, I had an aunt who could do that when she sang," exclaimed Ernie, "but what has it got to do with Long-Toed Poggles?"

"They shattered them!" cried Norman, barely able to control his tears now.

"Yes, Poggle," the Professor nodded gravely. "I'm afraid they did. Somehow the Drones worked out that each Poggle had its own special note. If they could tune into it and reproduce it at the right pitch and intensity, the poor thing would literally be shaken to death. The Drones killed hundreds in this way. They would lurk in the shadows then surround individuals and begin to hum – low at first, then gradually rising up the scale until they sensed they had found the weakness. Once they had, the group would drone louder and louder until it was all over. The Poggles didn't stand a chance, and soon there were only a handful left, deep underground."

"What happened next?" Norm and Ern blurted together.

"Well, that's the strange thing. The last few Poggles remained hidden for months, too scared to go above the surface where they knew the Drones were living on the Dark Side. They thought it was only a matter of time until they were discovered, deep in their tunnels, and killed. Days passed, though, and the Drones didn't come. Then one day a Poggle called Scott couldn't take being cooped up anymore and announced that he was going above. The rest of the Poggles pleaded with him not to go to his certain death, but Scott said he would rather die above ground in the light than wait to be killed in the dark. A few hours later, he returned to the group with the news that the Drones had gone. They had simply disappeared, and to this day no one knows why."

Norm and Ern felt as though they had been caught up in a fantastic bedtime story only to find that the last page had been torn from the book.

"It can't end like that," Norm said, almost crossly. "What happened to the rest of the Poggles?"

"Well, they rebuilt their lives and gradually repaired the damage to the Planet. Eventually, things began to return to normal and the numbers of Poggles increased; however, Poggles were no longer born with long toes, almost as if they had evolved to protect themselves against possible extinction again."

Norm gasped. "I can hardly believe this is all true," he sighed, "but it explains so much. If only I knew how to control what I feel and use it the way the old Long-Toed Poggles did. If anything, I think I'm falling over more than ever these days."

"Yes, well, you would be." Professor Zube stopped picking up shards of glass and looked calmly at the two Poggles. "You see, the Drones are back."

At the Professor's feet, a small ball of fluff turned from orange to pure white.

A FLASH OF
LIGHT

IT WAS A LONG NIGHT.

The two friends continued to question the Professor until nearly three in the morning when he insisted they went home to their pods. Not, however, before he explained, to their horror, how the Drones had regrouped. The Professor had been monitoring the Dark Planet for years through his telescope, even though it was understood to be deserted. Three months ago, he had seen signs of life once more. The Drones were back and, worse still, they were building something.

Neither Norm nor Ern slept at all when they eventually crept back into their beds. Yet both of them surprised their parents by being up and dressed before their alarms went off. In contrast to the previous morning, Norman fairly wolfed down his Wartflakes while trying to work out how he could smuggle Spong out of his bedpod. The little creature had been squeaking excitedly under his bed since his return. (Scheherazade had been most pleased to see him again and hear about his trip to the Wasteland.) There was no way Norman could explain to his parents how his pet had mysteriously returned in the middle of the night.

How did my life get so complicated? he thought as he gently coaxed Spong into his bubble bag a few moments later. *One minute I'm an ordinary Poggle – or rather, a long-toed, clumsy one – next, I'm having midnight feasts with Human Beings and learning about wars and invasions. Oh, and apparently I have special toes, too. It's ridiculous!*

Norm tried to sound indignant at the situation thrust upon him; but since hearing the Professor's words the night before, he felt the seed of something he had never experienced before. It was the warm feeling of knowing you had a fantastic secret all to yourself. He liked it.

Ernie was hopping anxiously from one foot to the other at the bottom of the path as, with a quick "Bye, then!", Norm let himself out of the house. Luckily his parents were too absorbed in frowning over a story in *The PUN* to notice his wriggling bubble bag.

"Crikey, I thought you'd never leave!" blurted Ern. "I've been waiting ages – didn't sleep a wink. Can't stop thinking about... you know..." He looked suspiciously over his shoulder at the hedge and remembered that they sometimes had ears.

"I know. I didn't sleep either. My head's buzzing like Fireflies around a syrup lake."

"Don't you mean, like insects around the Waste Dome?" joked Ernie, but neither of them felt like laughing at the memory of the sight and stench they had seen last night.

As they rounded the corner Ern stopped. "Hadn't you better let Spong out of your bag?"

An impatient series of squeaks from inside confirmed that this would be a good idea. Soon the orange creature was once more straining at his leash and leading the way to the school pod.

The path became crowded with the usual throng of Poggles shoving, dawdling and laughing to their daily routine. Norman and Ernie followed in thoughtful silence.

"You two idiots had a row, then?" Jeli Mould's whiney voice broke the spell.

Norm had completely forgotten to worry about the ritual bullying he suffered every day – somehow it had lost its importance. He stared blankly at Jeli and before she had time to line up another insult, a commotion broke out ahead of them. She turned in time to see Boris Whinge being frogmarched through the school pod gates on the arm of Bert Snatchitt.

"What the...?!" she blurted, and ran after the protesting Boris.

Norm and Ern exchanged wry smiles and quickened their pace. They reached the gates just in time to hear Bert retort to Jeli:

"None of your business, young Poggle, and none of *his* business to be sneaking about last night either!"

"That's shocking!" Ernie cried with dramatic exaggeration.

"Terrible!" Norm nodded, with a disappointed 'tut-tut' to Boris.

"But... but you... I heard... I was trying to..." Boris complained weakly, realising if he finished any of his sentences he would have to admit he'd been spying on them. Bert dragged him inside.

"Not a bad start to the day." Ernie winked.

Inside their classpod the usual clatter of bags and stools was in progress. Norm put Spong into his large pen and topped up his food and water. Ernie was on Fred-feeding duty that day, and he scooped some brown sludge from a jar into the Baracs Beetle's cage.

Norm grimaced, "I suppose that's p—"

"Dung, yes," interjected Ernie. "Fred's favourite."

"Well, he'd have a field day at the Waste Dome, then," Norm whispered under his breath, watching the insect gorge itself on the sticky mess.

"I think even Fred would be hard pushed to tackle that lot," mused Ern. "At least he'd never go hungry."

Miss Lastic arrived and the class settled down for the daily roll call.

"Norm *and* Spong today, I see," she said when she reached his name. "Are you sure he's fully recovered though, Norman? He still looks a little off colour to me. What did the vet say?"

"The vet? Ow! Oh yes, the vet!" Norm added quickly as Ernie's well-placed foot reminded him just in time of the story he had told Miss Lastic. "Just-a-bug-should-be-fine-in-no-time-nothing-to-worry-about," he garbled.

Another hard stare from Miss Lastic and a pause that seemed to last for an age. "I see," was all she said.

"Boris Whinge." Miss Lastic now directed her stare behind Norm's head.

"Yes, Miss Lastic?" Boris mumbled grudgingly.

"On report from Bert Snatchitt, I hear, Boris? Very disappointing. Not the sort of behaviour I'd expect from a

Poggle who has been given the honour of playing solo in front of the Elders. You'll see me after school today."

Boris flushed red and scowled.

"Now, class, speaking of our Elder Poggles," Miss Lastic glanced towards the corridor and nodded, "we are very honoured this morning to have a visitor."

A hushed silence fell immediately, and the class, without need for prompting, all stood as Ilona Quinn, one of the seven Elder Poggles, glided in. Of course, she was walking, really – Elder Poggles don't have wheels – but she did so with such effortless grace, appearing to look at every Poggle in the room at the same time with her gentle, all-knowing eyes. She stood in front of the class and drew her cloak around her. It was a plain brown cloak which had been painstakingly embroidered with an intricate pattern of ivy leaves.

"Good morning, Poggles, and be seated," she greeted them in the traditional way.

The class sat in awe and waited eagerly. Miss Lastic raised a questioning eyebrow to the Elder, who nodded with a smile.

"Class, Ilona Quinn is here today to very kindly take questions from us so that we may learn from her." The class gasped and a sea of hands shot into the air but Miss Lastic added, "Now, this is a unique opportunity and you will think carefully about the questions you ask so as not to waste this precious time. How much will you learn by simply knowing a person's favourite food or Telescreen programme when there are far greater questions you could ask?" Half of the hands went down and Miss Lastic scanned the faces in front of her.

"Anna Conda, you may ask your question."

Anna stood nervously and began in a faltering voice, "Elder Quinn... how... how do..." she tailed off.

Ilona Quinn smiled. "Take a deep breath, young Poggle. Just imagine you are talking to your friend in the playpod."

Anna nodded and began again. "How do you become an Elder Poggle, please. I mean, what exams would I need to take?" She sat down with a bump and a flushed face.

"That is a good question, Anna, and I shall try to give you a good answer." Ilona paused. "I'm afraid you cannot become an Elder by simply passing exams – it is not that easy." The class exchanged puzzled glances on hearing exams being referred to as 'easy'.

"To become an Elder requires effort – great effort. More than just looking at a Data-Globe and writing an essay," she smiled. "It is a long journey and there is more than one pathway. Some have become Elders through the wisdom and patience required to teach others." Ilona Quinn glanced at Miss Lastic, who looked surprised and blushed.

"Others have been chosen for their courage – fighting bravely to overcome public or personal battles that you and I may never see. There are also those who travel the path of compassion. They have the gift of thinking of others and lending a helping hand, wherever and however it is needed." The Elder Poggle paused and seemed far away for a moment.

Anna Conda couldn't help herself from blurting out, "But where do I start?" She suddenly felt she would do anything to become an Elder.

"Small things every day, Anna," replied Ilona gently. "You could start by being the first person up in the morning and making your family a cup of tea."

"What – *every* day?" asked Anna incredulously.

"*Every* day," said the Elder, with a twinkle in her eye. "I told you it wouldn't be easy."

Anna sat down, thinking how hard it would be to get up early on *one* day, let alone every day for the rest of her life. Surely it couldn't be that difficult? In her heart, though, she knew Ilona Quinn was right.

"Next question from... ah, yes... Norman Snodgrass." Miss Lastic nodded encouragingly at him.

Ernie gasped as his friend stood beside him. Usually, Norm wouldn't say boo to a Marge Fly, never mind stand up and ask a question of an Elder Poggle.

Norm cleared his throat and found he was able to look Ilona Quinn in the eyes without fear. He sensed she would wait patiently for as long as it took for him to find the right words. She was willing his question from him.

"Elder Quinn, please may I ask what you know about the Drones?"

A hushed silence fell on the class, but behind him Boris Whinge whispered, "Trust you to ask a stupid question about a fairy story."

Miss Lastic shot a worried glance at the Elder Poggle. "I'm... I'm not sure if we have time to answer that one..." she began, but the Elder raised her hand and Miss Lastic was quiet.

"We have time," she said simply. "Norman, is it? Where did you hear about the Drones?"

Norman swallowed. "A friend told me about them and how they invaded our Planet many years ago. I wondered if you could tell us more?" He managed to speak despite the fact that next to him Ern was squashing his toes, desperately trying to silence him. Barely stifled sniggers were erupting from Whinge & Co behind him.

"I wish I could tell you that they *were* the things of fairy tales," Ilona's eyes were sad as they rested on Boris Whinge, who was immediately quiet, "but your friend is right. Drones are part of our history and are part of our reality now. What must be, must be, and we cannot change that. Warriors have fought them in the past and new Warriors will be called upon in the future… although they may not know it yet."

"… new Warriors will be called upon in the future…"

These words had the strangest effect on Norman, who felt as if he wanted to run far away, yet at the same time fight anything in his path. For some reason, the Elder Poggle was gazing at his toes. They began to tingle.

"Thank you, Elder Quinn." He sat down.

"We have time for one final question, I believe... Well, alright then, Boris Whinge." Miss Lastic grudgingly gave Boris the floor.

"What *is* your favourite Telescreen programme?"

Norman was grateful that hooting practice had been stepped up a gear due to the forthcoming anniversary celebrations. Both Ernie and Boris were called away during break time, and he was able to find a quiet bench in the playpod to think. He found himself repeating the words of the Elder Poggle over and over in his head.

'Drones are part of our reality... What must be, must be... may not know it yet...'

He had the uneasy feeling that her words had been aimed at him. It made him very uncomfortable. What with the Professor going on about his toes, and now this. He felt as if he were being prodded into the centre of a huge stage and he wasn't at all sure what his lines were or what the play was all about. He had a nasty feeling that the Drones were a part of it, though.

He shook his head. "Come on, Norm, snap out of it," he told himself. "You're thinking crazy thoughts. Everyone knows you're more of a worrier than a Warrior!" He chuckled over his own joke as he made his way to his next lesson.

Astronomy with Mr Astra was normally an enjoyable subject. Mr Astra's Data-Helmet would produce a myriad of twinkling stars, planets and asteroids, which whirled gracefully above his head while he identified various interesting features in a soothing voice. By the end of a lesson, the class was usually calm and a little sleepy.

Comets were today's subject, and a bright white flash of light made a perfect orbit around Mr Astra's ears as he spoke.

"Now, a comet is really a big chunk of ice with a tail – usually made up of a load of dust it is dragging behind it. You might call it a dirty snowball, in fact."

Norman didn't think this was a very flattering description for the beautiful streak of light brightening the entire classpod.

"When the comet's orbit takes it towards any bright star, like our Sirius or the Earth's Sun, its tail blazes as you see now. They normally pass every hundred years or so but of course we don't usually see them."

"Why not, Mr Astra?" Theresa Green posed the question.

"Well, you would need to see the sky in the dark to be able to view them and, of course, we Poggles live on the Light Side of our Planet where it never gets fully dark, even in our night-time. The only way for us to see them would be to go to the Dark Side – but I wouldn't recommend it." Mr Astra laughed nervously.

"Luckily for us, we do have a record of the last time a comet passed us, and if you select screen seven hundred and thirty-three on your Data-Globes you can read an account of it that was filed at the time."

The class busied themselves with button-pushing and scrolling through menus. Words floated in the air past Norm's nose and an image of a huge comet appeared. He read, with waning interest, of how one had passed extremely near to the

Dark Side of the Planet almost a hundred years ago. It had been almost as bright as the Dog Star itself.

Norm felt his eyelids droop as the report went on to describe, in great detail, the different types of comets, the structure of their tails and whatnot. He scanned down to the bottom of the page where the last word caught his eye. Scott. The report had been written by a Poggle called Scott. For some reason this fact began itching away at Norm's brain as if it ought to mean something. He glanced at Ernie to see if he'd noticed anything but Ern was already on the next screen and reading on obliviously. Norm shook his head to clear it and the niggling thought went away.

The rest of the day passed quickly, although just as Norm was leaving, Miss Lastic reminded him pointedly about his homework deadline. "The end of the week is tomorrow, don't forget. No excuses this time."

"Tell you what, Norm," whispered Ern sympathetically after she had gone, "why don't we pop up to the surface after tea? We can grub around for a bit then see what we can find?"

"Thanks, Ern," Norm replied gratefully.

The light was already fading to twilight, as dark as it ever got on this side of the Planet, when the Poggles, accompanied by a contented Spong, reached the surface. They decided that a trip to the Wasteland was probably out of the question at this hour. Neither of them really felt like experiencing the smell again, although their new friend, the Professor, had invited them to drop in at any time.

They set to. Ern began prodding rocks and poking enthusiastically at the green dust beneath. Norm made a show of searching but found himself rather too preoccupied with the day's events to concentrate. As the light faded further, Ern unclipped a jar of Firelighters from his utility belt and shone it into the dark cracks and crevices of a large rock. A moth-like insect appeared and bumbled around the jar, banging its head as it did so. Ern tried to shoo it away but it persisted and flew up his hooter, making him sneeze.

"Stupid thing." He sneezed again. The bedraggled moth reappeared and fluttered off hastily, to dry its damp wings. Ern carried on searching while Norm watched from a safe distance over his shoulder, still deep in thought. The sound of chuckling roused him from his ponderings.

"What is it, Ern?"

"Look at this!"

Norm and Spong watched as Ernie lifted a small stone and shone the Firelighter on a purple beetle that was now frantically trying to dodge the beam of light directed at it. Ern herded it into a small pen of sand he had created but it ran nimbly over the top and dived for the nearest stone again.

"Hee-hee, you can't escape that easily," he chuckled as he lifted the lid off the creature's world once more and sent it scuttling across the dust. Spong strained on his leash, eager to sniff and investigate.

"Why do you think it's behaving like that, Norm?" Ernie tried to engage his half-interested friend in conversation.

"I don't know," Norm replied absent-mindedly. "Maybe it's just afraid of the light." As soon as the words left his mouth he felt as if a huge comet had made a detour on its orbit and had shot between his ears, lighting up the darkest corners of his fuzzy brain. He understood now why ideas were sometimes drawn as light bulbs above the head.

"Eureka!" he yelled, startling his friend so badly that he dropped the Firelighters. The purple beetle shot off as fast as its legs could carry it, and Spong squeaked excitedly.

"You what?!" cried Ern in fright, looking around wildly for a clue to Norm's sudden outburst.

"Eureka!" Norm repeated, grinning and dancing on the spot. "I've got it! They're afraid of the light!" He skipped around again like a maniac, then stood stock still. "We have to tell Professor Zube!" And before Ernie could say another word, his once sane friend disappeared off in the direction of the nearest Zube Tube.

Ernie had no choice but to follow.

A CUNNING PLAN

TEN MINUTES LATER, Ern was still bewildered. Norman had been rambling on since they'd got there. At first the Professor had been preoccupied with his experiments, staring despondently first at the model of the Waste Dome, then at the green globe in his hand which had even more brown sludge inside it. Gradually, Professor Zube began to register what Norm was saying, and he turned to listen intently to his visitor.

Suddenly there was a shout of, "Great Scott! Of course!" and the two of them quite frankly became as bad as each other.

They were now dancing around and flapping their arms like demented chickens, with Spong jumping up to join in the excitement.

Poor Ernie felt like an outsider at a brilliant party. He had no idea why they were making such a fuss about a stupid beetle that didn't like the light – it was ridiculous.

At last he'd had enough and said quite crossly, "Will someone *please* tell me what on the Planet is going on?"

Norm and the Professor spun round. They had almost forgotten Ernie was there.

"Great Scott! Of course!"

"I'm sorry," his friend apologised. "I've been so desperate to talk to the Professor, I haven't explained anything to you – you must think we've gone mad."

"I am a little puzzled, I'll admit." Ernie didn't have the nerve to say he thought they were both bonkers.

"Well, it's like this…" Norm began, "I've had a fuzzy head all day…"

His friend resisted mumbling, 'So, what's new?'

Norm continued, "I mean, obviously I've been thinking about what happened last night and what the Professor said about the Drones being back – but it's more than that. There's what Elder Quinn said about them as well – how they were part of our reality, as well as our history, and what must be, must be. She knew they would be coming back, too – it's inevitable." Norm looked encouragingly at his friend, who was still none the wiser.

"I don't see why that makes you happy, though," he said with a shrug.

"Well, then there was Mr Astra's class today where we learned about comets." Ern continued to look blank. "I just had the feeling that there was something important about them coming around every hundred years or so – but I didn't know why. Then I spotted the name of the Poggle who had seen the last comet and that started going around in my head, too."

"Who was it?" Ern asked quickly.

"Scott!" Norm said triumphantly.

"Wait a minute…" Ernie paused, "wasn't he one of the last Long-Toed Poggles who survived the Great War? The one who went up to the surface to face the Drones?" Ern was getting excited too.

"Yes!" cried Norm. "Exactly!"

"But… but…" Ernie looked crestfallen. "Nope, I still don't get it," he sighed.

The Professor chuckled quietly and nodded at Norman to go on.

"It was actually you who solved the mystery for me," Norm said to his friend kindly. "It was when you were playing with that beetle on the surface and you asked me why it ran away from the light."

"Yes, and you said it must be afraid of it but – so what?" Ern was still grasping at straws.

"Well, it suddenly came to me that if a tiny bug can be afraid of the light, why can't bigger things be afraid of the light too? Drones, for instance. It would have to be a really bright light to scare them off, though… something massive, like—"

"A comet!" shrieked Ern, finally catching on.

"You've got it!" cried Norm, waltzing his friend up and down the room delightedly. "The comet scared them off! Drones are afraid of the light!"

"Oh, my clever young Poggles – I think you could be right. It would certainly explain why they live on the Dark Planet and took over the Dark Side of ours. Now, to check the facts…" He skipped off down the room to a shelf of books and ran his finger along them, sending dust flying into the air. "A… B… C… Yes, here we are – Curries, Comets… This is it." He skipped back towards them, leafing through the book. "Scott was right – a massive comet called Hiya Pop was seen from Earth at the same time as Scott reported his sighting. Whew!" the Professor whistled. "What a brave Poggle he was. Not only did he leave the safety of underground, but he must have travelled to the Dark Side as well in his search for the Drones. Yes, the dates all tie in with the end of the Great War, ninety-six years ago!" The Professor grabbed the two small Poggles by the arm and danced them around the room again, knocking over several piles of papers as he spun them.

Finally they collapsed, exhausted, into the comfy armchairs, and the Professor chatted breathlessly.

"Oh, it's not a moment too soon. I'm so glad you came straight here and told me. You see, I've worked out what the Drones are building and it's not good news."

Norm and Ernie stopped grinning.

"A UV ray, of course."

The Poggles looked blank.

"Goodness me, the schools these days – surely Mr Ree has covered this in Science? U–V… ultra violet? No?"

Norm and Ern squirmed and both felt as if they were failing this examination dismally.

"Is it something to do with rainbows?" Ern had a flash of memory.

"Indeed it is, Poggle! Richard of York Gave Battle in Vain! I've lost you again, haven't I?"

The Poggles nodded; they hadn't a clue who this Richard of York chappie was or what he had to do with rainbows.

"It's quite simple. You know what the colours of the rainbow are – Red, Orange, Yellow, Green, Blue, Indigo and Violet – well, ROYGBIV is a bit hard to memorise, so that's why we use the Richard of York thingy – it's called a *mnemonic*, which is just a fancy way of saying 'something you make up to help you remember something else'. I use 'em all the time. For instance, I never leave the house until I've had a SPIT." Two bemused faces stared at him. "Socks, Pants, Itching Powder and Trousers, of course – can't leave home without those!"

Considering Poggles didn't wear pants or trousers, this did nothing to enlighten them and, quite frankly, had Professor Zube forgotten these on Earth, someone would have reminded him pretty quickly, so it was a poor example all round. Neither could they fathom out why a full-grown person would need itching powder – but they were too polite to ask.

"Well, never mind about that. The point is, we can see the colours of the rainbow and when you mix them all up they make white light (it's true, Dear Reader, try it), which of course is no good for Drones. So, they use ultraviolet – invisible light waves that they can see quite clearly with their specially adapted eyes. It's a bit like wearing night-vision goggles. Anyway," (sensing he had lost them once more) "the Drones use these UV rays to see where they're going. The further they need to travel, the stronger the UV rays they need. Judging by the size of the construction going on, I'd say they're planning quite a journey."

Norm and Ernie gulped. Neither of them wanted to ask the obvious question on their minds. The Professor answered it anyway.

"I think you both know what this means," he said solemnly. "The ray is pointing directly towards the Dark Side of our Planet, and by the look of it it's nearly finished."

It was a while before anyone spoke. The realisation of the impending horror made speech impossible. The Poggles simply sat, blinking rapidly. Finally, Professor Zube stood and broke the silence.

"We need a plan – and fast," he said, striding over to a workbench nearby and proceeding to search in the various wooden drawers and boxes around it. In no time, the bench was littered with light bulbs, candles, ping-pong balls, string, rubber bands and anything else the Professor could lay his hands on. He began connecting rubber bands together, then shook his head and took them apart again. Next, he lit the candle and stared at it for a full five minutes without moving. Suddenly, he sprang into life and started making scribbled notes in a book while muttering to himself.

Norman and Ernie exchanged glances, not sure whether to stay or go. The muttering and scribbling continued, then Professor Zube fished a strange looking light on a piece of thick elastic out of a drawer and proceeded to strap it onto his head. On Earth, these contraptions are common, especially in mines where the miners attach them to their helmets so they have their hands free to work in the dark. The Sugar Rock miners on the Green Planet would have laughed their socks off at this (had they worn socks). Their daily work was well lit by the swarms of Firelighters which were attracted to the sugary walls of the mine.

The Professor switched the light on and started moving his head from side to side, watching the beam and making notes. Ernie was beginning to get bored. He picked up a small object from a nearby bench and began fiddling. It had a glass dial with the numbers one to twelve around it. In its surface he could see another laboratory reflected back at him, with a miniature Professor Zube working at a scaled-down bench. Ernie twisted the object so he could see Norm in the glass, staring at his toes. As he moved the reflection back to Professor Zube, the light from the Professor's headlamp caught the dial and bounced onto the walls of the Laboratory. Ernie smiled and spent the next few moments happily directing the spot of light around the room, up and down the bookcases and across the rows of coloured jars which lit up like traffic lights in turn.

Seeing the light, Spong gave chase, and Ernie quite forgot his two companions were there as he sent the little creature whizzing round faster and faster until—

"Eureka!" shouted the Professor, shielding his eyes from the glare from the watch (for that is what the object was).

"Oh, sorry!" gabbled Ern. "I didn't mean to shine it in your eyes; I was just…"

"You fantastic Poggles! You've done it again!" continued the Professor.

Once more, Ern and Norm exchanged bewildered looks. The Professor skipped over and held Ern's arm up in the air. "Hold it there... That's it, don't move!" he beamed. The Professor moved his head from side to side until the light from his headlamp caught the watch. "Oh, yes, fantastic... and so simple! Why didn't I see it before?" He threw himself down in his chair again and began crossing out diagrams and scribbling furiously.

"Er... Professor... are you OK?" asked Norm.

"Oh, my goodness yes, young Poggle. Never been better. Once again you have come up with the answer to the problem – here, let me explain." He stood and wiped some markings off a board on the wall.

"Now, we've identified that Drones are afraid of the light, haven't we?"

Norm and Ernie nodded.

"Good. And we know that the Drones are building a UV ray so they can invade the Dark Side of the Green Planet again?"

More nods and worried stares.

"So, the problem is how to get light over to the Dark Side to scare them off when they get here."

The Poggles looked bemused.

"Well, thanks to Ernie, we have the solution!"

More confused looks.

"Come, come, it's simple really." He drew a circle on the board. "Here's the Green Planet (scribble), here's us on the Light Side, and there's the Dark Side (scribble, scribble). Now, where do we get our light from?"

Norm and Ern felt like they were back in Mr Astra's Astronomy class.

"From the Dog Star," they chorused.

"Good," said Professor Zube. He drew the Dog Star above the Green Planet. "Now, if we use the principle of reflection that Ernie showed us just now, we can use the light from the Dog Star and move it over to the Dark Side using a system of mirrors."

"Mirrors?" queried Ern.

"Yes. As you know, light will only travel in a straight line and doesn't usually like to bend around corners, right?"

"Ooh, ooh, yes! Mr Ree taught us that in Science the other week!" exclaimed Norm, delighted to have understood something at last.

"Right! Well, if someone was to stand on the Light Side of the Planet and hold a big mirror up, they could reflect the light of the Dog Star to somewhere else." He drew a small Poggle on the Light Side, holding a mirror, and a straight line to show the path of light bouncing off.

"As you can see, one mirror would only reflect the light in a straight line and, as we know, the Green Planet is round, so to get the light around the corner, so to speak, we need more mirrors!" He drew a stick figure standing further round the Planet where the Dark Side met the Light. Then he angled the ray to hit the mirror above its head and reflect round to the Dark Side. Finally, he drew another figure standing on the Dark Side whose mirror reflected the light upwards. "Right! Any questions?" grinned the Professor.

"Yes. Can I put my arm down now, please?" asked Ern wincing.

"Goodness, yes! Have you been holding it up all this while? Give it a shake to get the feeling back."

Whilst the Professor revived Ernie's numb arm, Norman continued to stare at the diagram on the board. An ominous thought was forming in his head. Was it his imagination, or was the figure standing on the Dark Side a little podgy with a slightly longer middle toe?

"Er, Professor," Norm hardly dared to ask the question "who is holding *that* mirror?"

"Ah. Well, it's funny you should ask that." The Professor crouched down so that his eyes met Norman's and, when he spoke, his voice was suddenly serious. "Norman, you are a very special Poggle – no, I know you don't feel it but, I promise you, it is no coincidence that a Long-Toed Poggle is in existence just at the time when the Green Planet is in grave danger."

Norman gulped. His heart was pounding and he suddenly felt very sick.

"Now, I know what I am asking of you is an enormous task… and you will have to be a very brave Poggle – just like Scott was – but Norman, I wouldn't ask you if I didn't think you could do it. I think you'll find you have more courage than you know."

A sharp intake of breath broke the silence as Ernie grasped what was going on. He tried to make up for it by offering some words of encouragement but he could only think with awe of the daunting task facing his friend.

Strangely, Norman didn't try to argue. The words of Ilona Quinn (was it only that morning she had spoken to him?) quietly replayed in his mind: 'Warriors have fought them in the past and new Warriors will be called on in the future… although they may not know it yet.' Somehow he knew she had meant him and, while every part of him wanted to run away back to his pod and pretend this was all a bad dream, he knew that his task was inevitable. *He* had to be the one to travel to the Dark Side. He took a large breath and gave a small nod of acceptance.

Professor Zube gave a sad-ish sort of smile in return. "You know it has to be you. With your extra-long toes, you're the only one who can sense the Drones arriving… At least you'll be ready for them…"

Behind the Professor, Norman could see his friend's eyes widen at the mention of the Drones' arrival, but he himself felt strangely numb.

"Don't worry, Poggle, you won't be entirely alone; you'll have Spong with you. He's a clever little animal and very useful when the going gets tough – you'll see." He ruffled Spong under the chin, and Spong licked his hand affectionately.

For a moment Norm wondered how the Professor knew so much about the class pet. He wished he'd asked Miss Lastic more about the creature and where he'd come from. Too late for that now, though.

"Well, now," the Professor straightened up and looked at his watch, "it's getting on, and you two had better head home before your folks wonder where you are. I need to work out the finer details of our plan. It will need some precise trigonometry if it's going to work."

"Trigger what?" Ern frowned.

"Trig-oh-nom-eh-tree… Don't tell me Miss Take hasn't taught you about it. Angles? Triangles? Hypotenuse…?"

"Oh yes, I think she mentioned something about that," Ern replied weakly, wondering what a hippopotamus had to do with it.

"Right, well, pop back tomorrow after school. I should have it all worked out by then."

The mention of school suddenly jogged Ernie's memory. "Oh Norm – we've forgotten your homework – it's meant to be ready for Miss Lastic tomorrow... We'll never find any bugs now!"

Norm found it difficult to share Ernie's concern about the unfinished homework. Faced with the prospect of tackling an army of invading Drones, an empty jam jar where his homework should be seemed insignificant. Rather like being in the path of a tidal wave and realising you've left the bath on at home. Miss Lastic probably wouldn't see it like that, though. Even if he tried to explain why the jam jar was empty again, there was no way she would believe him. He would never hear the end of it from Boris either. Norm shrugged helplessly.

"What's this about homework?" asked the Professor.

"We were meant to find some bugs to study in class this week," explained Ern, "only Norm broke his jam jar when Spong escaped. Miss Lastic's given him till the end of the week to hand his in – only that's tomorrow..." Ern glanced nervously at Norm.

"Bugs, eh..." said Professor Zube with a slight smile, "and I suppose the rarer the better?"

"Oh yes," nodded Ern. "I found a Trojan!" he added proudly, unable to help himself.

"Well, I think I might be able to help you there, Norm." Professor Zube turned and reached over to a ledge behind the model of the Waste Dome that neither Norm nor Ern had noticed before. He gently lifted down a glass tank in which, to their amazement, was a shiny Baracs Beetle.

"Fred!" exclaimed the Poggles in unison.

"Fred?" said Professor Zube with a puzzled look. "You mean Ginger. He's the only surviving Baracs Beetle on the Planet, I'm afraid. Been trying to find him a mate but… well, under the circumstances I think you deserve to have him for your homework, Norm."

"But he's not the last!" beamed Norm. "We've got one in our classpod – Fred! They'll be able to have babies!"

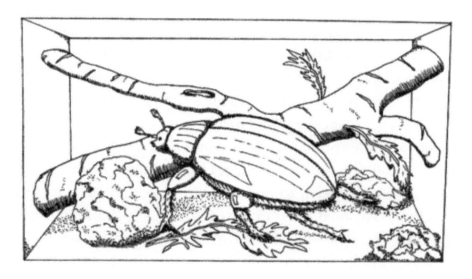

"a shiny Baracs Beetle…"

"Only one problem with that," grimaced Ern as he peered intently at Ginger's undercarriage. "Fred and Ginger are both boys."

"Oh." Norm was crestfallen. "Well, at least they'll be good company for each other for a while. Miss Lastic will be chuffed."

The Professor carefully lifted Ginger out of his tank and coaxed him into Norm's jam jar, sealing the lid tightly.

"Now, take good care of him, Norm," he instructed.

"Oh, I promise I will." Norm held the jar up to his face and watched the precious beetle exploring the few grains of dirt in the bottom. *Boris will never believe this,* he thought, and for a moment he brightened and forgot the awful task that lay ahead.

A STRANGE MEETING

NORM'S CHANGE OF MOOD DIDN'T LAST LONG. Back in his pod he carefully put Ginger's jar under his bed and slipped into the kitchen where his parents were having supper. He had almost run straight in to show them the Baracs Beetle but realised it would involve a lot of explaining – or more lies. Thankfully, they were distracted by seeing Spong looking so well recovered from his 'trip to the vet'.

As Spong bounced around happily, performing tricks for morsels of sugarloaf, Norm reflected on how complicated life had become. He toyed with his mug of night tea and only managed a bite of his toast. Arthur Snodgrass gave him a look of concern.

"Why don't you get an early night, Norm?" he said gently. "I think you've been feeding the Firelighters at both ends – it'll do you good."

For once Norman didn't argue, and with a nod mumbled, "Night, then…" and shuffled off to his bedpod.

An hour later he was still wide awake and staring at the ceiling. *Madness*, he thought to himself. *Utter madness to believe I can do this. What was I thinking? Going to the Dark Side on my own will be bad enough… but tackling the Drones… What if I'm shattered?* His head began to throb and his toes tingled unpleasantly. Norm sighed.

A sliver of light pierced the darkness as his father peered round the bedpod door.

"You alright, Son? I thought I heard a noise."

The huge lump in his throat choked any reply Norm could make. Arthur Snodgrass was no fool and could sense a troubled soul in need of comfort.

"Did I tell you the funny thing that happened at work today?" he said as he sat on his son's bed. Without waiting for a reply, he continued, "Well, we were down at the face of the Sugar Rock Mine… found a lovely tasty seam, and we'd been picking away at it for a while. The Sweep Team were following behind us collecting up all the small lumps and dust for processing, the way they do. Anyway, there's this one Poggle, Robbie his name is – always complaining about something. Well, he's lagging behind the sweepers, fussing with his broom and grumbling away to himself about something or other. In the end he marches right up to the boss, and do you know what he says?"

Norm shook his head.

"*It's no good,* he says, *there's something wrong with this broom… Three times the handle's come out and now the head's fallen off!*" Arthur Snodgrass wheezed with uncontrollable laughter. "Do you get it, Son? Three times the handle… and now the head…? Oh, you couldn't write it…"

At the sound of his father's laughter, the lump in Norman's throat loosened its grip. "Dad," he said, "can I ask you a question?"

"Of course you can, Norm," his father replied, wiping the tears from his eyes. "What is it?"

"Supposing... hypothetically, of course... that you had to make a choice about whether to do something... difficult, or not, how would you know what to do?"

Norman's father let his gaze rest on his son for a while. "Now, that's a good question, Norm... a very good question... one we all have to ask ourselves from time to time. I reckon, deep down, you probably know the answer already."

"But I don't," Norm protested weakly.

"It's quite simple, really," his father continued. "You just have to do what you believe to be right... but make sure you do it for the right reasons. That's all."

Norman frowned, so his father continued, "Take today, for instance – I felt a bit sorry for Robbie after the fiasco with his broom, so when we stopped for tea I fixed it up with a bit of old wire I keep in my pocket. You never know when it'll come in useful. The things I've made out of old wire – I could write a book! Anyway, unbeknown to me, Robbie showed the boss my handiwork. He was so impressed, he asked me to do a bit of overtime and modify all the brooms. There's a design fault, and they're all like it, apparently."

"That's great, Dad, but I still don't understand what you mean." Norm was confused.

"Well, if I'd have thought to myself, *I know, if I help Robbie out, he'll tell the boss and I'll get some overtime*, I'd have been doing the right thing but for the wrong reason – do you see?"

"Yes, but what if you r-really don't know what the right thing is in the first place?" Norm's voice cracked with emotion again.

"Ah, there's an easy answer to that as well, but you probably won't like it."

Norm swallowed the lump that was rising in his throat again.

His father continued, "If you're faced with two choices but don't know which is the right one, you'll usually find it's the hardest of the two, I'm afraid."

Yet, rather than alarm Norman, these words had the same effect on him as those spoken by Ilona Quinn earlier that day. The simple truth of them struck him and gave him the sense that he was just a small cog in a very big wheel, a wheel whose every turn was being planned and monitored by brains far greater than his and that, somehow, all would be well.

"OK, thanks, Dad," he smiled gratefully.

"Anytime, Son. Now, talking of old wire, I've an idea for Spong's cage. We can rig up an automatic feeding system if we get two lengths of wire, a spring and a..." But before he could finish his sentence, Norm had drifted into a deep, dreamless sleep.

"Norm had drifted into a deep, dreamless sleep."

Beneath Norman's bed, four pairs of eyes widened in delight.

"Forgive me staring but I never thought I'd see a Baracs Beetle again!" Sherri moved closer to the jar Norman had hidden. "My name is Scheherazade, but you can call me Sherri – I'm delighted to meet you. You must have quite a tale to tell."

Ginger did. In the quiet darkness he told Sherri his life story. He spoke of happy days spent scuttling around the planet with his many friends, and dark times as, one by one, they had all died of starvation. He explained how the waste-pipe system had destroyed their only means of finding food. The pipes whisked it all to the Waste Dome where it simply fermented and became poisonous. In desperation, Ginger had followed one of the pipes to the Wasteland, where Professor Zube had found him and taken him in.

Sherri was horrified, but Ginger had more to tell. By the time he'd finished, the Scudder knew all the details of Professor Zube's plan and the part Norman was to play in it. Sherri thanked Ginger sadly and climbed onto Norman's pillow. Gently, she whispered her most comforting stories into his ear as he slept.

Norm felt like a different Poggle in the morning. Firstly, it was a beautiful day. Even though it was never fully dark on the Light Side of the Planet, the green morning glow from Sirius had a certain quality to it that always lifted his spirits as it filtered through the Zube Tube openings close to the surface.

Then there was the fact that he would be marching proudly into class with his trump card to play. He chuckled happily as he fed Ginger a few globs of dung from the bottle Professor Zube had given him.

I can't wait to see the look on Boris's smug face! he thought as he did a little jig round his bedpod, sending Ginger spinning round the jar, waving his feelers in protest.

"Whoops, sorry, Ginge! Didn't mean to give you a headache."

The disgruntled beetle wiped some smears of dung off its shell with its back legs and began to digest them.

"Crikey, I never realised how much you beetles ate," Norm marvelled, as he poured the last dregs of dung into the jar. "This bottle was full last night!"

Seeing the creature gorging itself suddenly reminded Norm that he was RAV-EN-OUS! He looked down at his stomach, which was slightly less podgy than usual. An empty rumbling from within reinforced the fact that he'd not had a good feed for days.

After two rounds of baked hasbeans on toast and a large mug of Mrs Snodgrass's famous pick-me-up tea, Norm felt almost like his old self. He clipped on Spong's lead and slipped Ginger into his bubble bag. Sensing Norm's change of mood, Spong trilled happily, and a few minutes later they were trotting off to school with Ernie.

A large crowd of Poggles gathered in the playpod and there was a chorus of 'oohs' and 'wows' as Norm held Ginger's jar aloft.

"Nice one, Norm!" The words of praise came from the unexpected voice of Jeli Mould.

"Th-thanks, Jeli," said Norm in amazement. Was Jeli blushing?!

"What? Is he your new boyfriend now or something?" Boris Whinge's voice was laden with sarcasm. "It's only a dumb beetle."

Jeli hung her head and slunk into the school pod behind him. Before Norman and Ernie could exchange thoughts about this curious incident, the bell rang and they were caught in the scrabble for the doors.

Miss Lastic's face was a picture when, a few moments later, Norm placed his jar of homework on the podium in front of her. It was several minutes before she could speak.

"Well," she gasped at last, "this is most unexpected. A Baracs Beetle! Where on the Green Planet did you find it?"

"Near the Wasteland," replied Norm truthfully. There were murmured whisperings from the rest of the class at this revelation – the Wasteland was not a popular destination. "But he's a boy like Fred," he added quickly before Miss Lastic jumped to the same wrong conclusion.

"Oh... well, that's a pity," she peered into the jar more closely, "but even so... two Baracs Beetles are far better than one! Why don't you introduce him to Fred?"

The class crowded over to Fred's tank and watched as Norm carefully lowered Ginger's jar into it. Fred appeared from behind his ball of breakfast dung sensing that something interesting was afoot. Slowly, Norm unscrewed the lid and stood back to observe.

At first neither beetle moved, but their antennae twitched as each picked up the other's scent. Gradually, Ginger crept out of his jar and inched towards Fred, feelers extended. Then

Fred crawled forward until their feelers touched – in the same way that humans might shake hands. Finally, with a little jump, Fred did an about-turn and scurried excitedly around the tank with Ginger in tow, almost as if he were giving his new friend a guided tour.

"That has to be worth an A star, Norman," beamed Miss Lastic. "Well done! Now, settle back into your seats, class; we've had enough excitement for now."

"S'not fair!" a familiar voice chipped in. "How come he gets full marks for handing it in late?" The complaining voice of Boris Whinge went unnoticed as the class booted up their Data-Globes.

Norm reluctantly tore his gaze away from the two happy beetles who were now side by side and tucking into a mound of fresh dung; but before he could switch on his Data-Globe, Miss Lastic addressed him again. "Norman, I need you to take this Thought Memo to the Star Chamber."

Everyone in the class stopped work and watched as Miss Lastic pushed a button on her Data-Helmet. A tiny cube was ejected from the side of it. She placed it into a small plastic bubble bag, sealed it and handed it to Norm.

"You may take Spong with you; he could do with the walk," she added.

Now there were loud whisperings around the room and glances of envy directed at him. It was very unusual for junior Poggles to be allowed into the Star Chamber outside of assembly hours, but to be excused classwork to walk the school pet was unheard of.

"Who should I give this to when I get there, Miss Lastic?" asked Norm, slightly apprehensively.

"You'll be met," was the simple reply.

With a wide-eyed glance at Ernie, Norm collected Spong and headed off.

Having been instructed to take Spong for a walk, Norm led the way into the nearest Poggle-made tunnel. Since the installation of the Zube Tube network, this ancient system had become almost disused. Only a few older Poggles, who were distrustful of modern inventions, trod the paths. The old tunnels now had a damp, musky smell, and Spong pulled this way and that, contentedly exploring the nooks and crannies as they walked.

Fortunately, the route to the chamber was clearly marked by star and arrow symbols etched into the walls at intervals. Norm's feet plodded on autopilot further into the centre of the Planet while his brain busied itself with this latest strange turn of events. He rolled the bubble bag around in his hand, wishing that he knew the contents of Miss Lastic's Thought Memo and wondering who it was for. Trying to mind-read it was useless – Thought Memos only opened when in the hands of their intended reader.

Deeper and deeper into the centre of the Planet they descended, their path now lit by jars of Firelighters.

"We must be getting close now, Spong," Norm whispered, afraid to disturb the dense silence around them. "We've been walking for ages."

Sure enough, as they turned the next bend they saw a star-shaped opening illuminated at the far end of the tunnel.

Without warning, a dark figure darted out of the shadows beside them and grabbed Norm by the hooter.

"a dark figure...
grabbed Norm by the hooter."

"What are you doing down here out of class?!" Bert Snatchitt demanded. He tightened his grip and made Norman's eyes water; but before he could answer, another shape slid into view.

"It's alright, Bert, he's with me. Let him go."

Bert spun round to find himself in the presence of none other than Zohar, the Master Poggle himself.

"S-sorry, Master," he stammered, trying to bow and salute at the same time. "I-I had no idea."

"That will do, Bert. I'm sure you're a busy Poggle and have somewhere you need to be." It was not a question but a quiet command. Bert hastily backed away down the tunnel, still bowing and muttering his apologies.

Norman found himself frozen in awe and unable to speak or move, but much to his embarrassment Spong was bouncing happily on the end of his lead. He jumped up at the Master's robes and squeaked excitedly.

Norm watched in disbelief as the Master picked the little creature up and allowed him to lick his face. For a moment, Master and Minky eyed each other, and an understanding seemed to pass between them. Zohar nodded, then gently placed Spong on the ground again, scratching him softly behind one of his small ears.

"Now, be good for your master," he said, before turning to Norm. "I believe you have something for me, Norman?"

"Y-yes, sir," Norman stuttered and held out the bubble bag awkwardly.

The Master Poggle took it, unzipped it and removed the little cube from inside. For a moment there was silence as the Elder Poggle focused intently on the cube. It shuddered and opened. A minute later, Zohar smiled and gave a satisfied nod.

"That is good news," was all he said.

Norm opened and shut his mouth, unsure whether he was supposed to say anything or simply leave. Nothing in his life had prepared him for this audience.

Zohar spoke: "And now I have something for you which I think you will find most helpful." Without waiting for a reply, the Master Poggle turned away from Norman and seemed to reach for something in the hem of his robe. He turned back and held out a small, round, shining object. "It's for your toe," he explained. "Your middle one."

"Th-thank you, sir!" exclaimed Norman, taking the gleaming trinket, which was in fact a ring. He examined it closely, noticing some strange marks and symbols engraved onto it.

Zohar continued, "It is a wave translator. When you wear it, it will help you to understand the vibrations you pick up. It should be useful for the task you have ahead of you..."

Norm inhaled sharply. "How do you know?" he blurted, quite forgetting who he was addressing.

Zohar smiled but his eyes were sad. "Put it on," he instructed gently.

Obediently, Norman bent down and slipped the ring onto the long, middle toe of his right foot. Spong sat patiently and watched. The ring fitted perfectly, and immediately Norman felt a curious sensation. His toes tingled, but now in a pleasant way, almost as if someone had tuned them. He no longer felt as if the slightest vibration would make him fall over. A wave of contentment flowed from his feet up his body, and he wiggled his toes happily, forgetting again whose company he was in.

"One last piece of advice... Watch out for their tails..."

Norm looked up to where the voice had come from, but Zohar had gone.

BAD TIMING

"**W**OW!" **EXCLAIMED ERNIE** in the playpod when he had finally been able to talk to his friend. "You met Zohar *and* he gave you a present?! What will Professor Zube say?"

"Ingenious!" said the Professor later that day as he held the toe-ring up to the light, squinting at it through an eyeglass. "It's a very sophisticated aerial... and there's something else I can't work out... Incredible! I never realised such advanced technology existed on the Green Planet. Judging by the hieroglyphs, it must be ancient! Well, it couldn't be better timing," he chuckled, and handed the ring back to Norman who quickly slipped it on again.

"How did Zohar know about our plan?" he asked.

"Hmm...? Oh, well, he *is* the Master Poggle, after all. I'm sure he has ways. Now, speaking of plans, we have work to do." Professor Zube smoothly changed the subject and led the way over to his workbench on which was an assortment of strange equipment.

"Right, let's recap." He held up a small figure with a large mirror taped to it. "Ernie, you will be stationed with mirror number one on the Light Side of the Planet at the closest point to Sirius. That way we will maximise the strength of the beam we have to work with. Using this protractor… yes, the thingy that measures angles… you will reflect the light at precisely ninety degrees towards me. I'll be stationed here with mirror number two, just beyond the Wasteland, where the Dark Side meets the Light." He picked up a larger figure and taped a second mirror to it.

"Got it!" said Ernie enthusiastically.

"Good. Now," the Professor continued, "I will capture your beam and, again using a protractor-thingy… Heavens, you've got me doing it now… using a *protractor*, I will send the light beam at ninety degrees over to Norman who will be waiting on the Dark Side."

Both Ernie and Professor Zube glanced at Norman, who calmly replied, "Got it."

The Professor took a third figure and taped a mirror to this as well. "Right, now, on my signal, Norm will capture my beam and direct the light upwards to the Dark Planet. If my calculations are right, the beam should be strong enough to light up a pretty large part of the surface. It'll give those old Drones the scare of their lives!"

With a chuckle, he clicked on his miner's headlamp that was now suspended above the work bench. A zig-zag of light hit the three figures before bouncing upwards onto a crude model of the Dark Planet, which was just a ping-pong ball painted black, hanging above the far end of the bench. "Hee-hee, they'll think twice before coming down here again!"

"Professor?" Norm interrupted him. "You said I should wait for your signal… but you'll be miles away. How will I know when it's time?"

"A-ha! Good question, young Poggle. Have you ever heard of walkie-talkies?"

"Walkie-whatties?" Norm frowned.

"Talkies," said the Professor. "Here, catch." He threw a small plastic object with two buttons and a long metal spike at Norman. "Now, go and stand in the airlock."

Norman dutifully shuffled off.

The Professor waited until he was out of hearing, then twiddled one of the knobs on his walkie-talkie and held it to his mouth. "Can you hear me, over?"

Ernie gasped as muffled crackles seemed to come out of the Professor's hand.

The airlock burst open and Norm rushed in.

"Wow! That was amazing! I could hear your voice inside this thing!"

"Yes, that's the idea," the Professor explained patiently. "You're meant to reply by holding this button down and talking in here. Now let's try again."

Norm hurried back to the airlock and the Professor's walkie-talkie crackled into life again.

"Can you hear me, Professor?" Norm's voice sounded tinny but no less excited.

"Roger, over," replied the Professor.

"Professor? It's Norm… Can you hear me?"

"Roger. I can hear you loud and clear," the Professor replied again.

The airlock opened once more and Norm emerged looking confused. "Who's Roger?" he asked.

"Dearie me." The Professor shook his head. "Roger is what you say instead of 'yes' when you're talking over the radio.

You say 'over' when you have finished so that the other person knows when to click their button to speak."

"Why don't you just say 'yes' and 'your turn'?" asked Ernie.

Now it was the Professor's turn to look puzzled.

"Do you know, I have absolutely no idea!" he laughed. "Anyway, let's get some practice in."

For the next hour, the three conspirators took it in turns to stand in the airlock and practise their 'Rogers' and 'overs' until they were perfect. Even Spong joined in by squeaking over the radio when he heard his name. Once the walkie-talkies were mastered, Professor Zube gave them reflection exercises using mirrors, torches and the protractor-thingies until they could quickly and accurately direct beams of light all over the laboratory.

There was a strange incident when Ernie's beam lit up the glass case containing the Professor's Waste Dome experiment. The Dome had stretched to twice its original size and was oozing horribly, when it suddenly imploded. The case shuddered and a muted 'whumpf' was heard through the thick glass. Brown toxic ooze seeped ominously over the surface of the model until nothing of the miniature Green Planet could be seen.

"What's happened to it, Professor?" asked Ernie, hoping it wasn't his fault.

"Nothing I haven't been expecting," the Professor replied with a frown, but before they could question him further he set them some more tasks.

Soon Norman and Ernie were worn out from sheer concentration, and Spong was exhausted from chasing spots of light all over the laboratory. The hard work paid off, though. The two friends were now able to angle their mirrors with remarkable speed and precision.

"By George, I think we're ready!" Professor Zube exclaimed at last.

"Who on the Planet is George?" the two Poggles groaned.

"Never mind that now," Professor Zube continued, "you both need to get a good night's sleep in readiness for tomorrow."

"Why, what's tomorrow?" Ernie asked nervously. He had a horrible feeling he knew the answer.

"Tomorrow…" said the Professor, bending down with an earnest gaze, "tomorrow is D-Day. Drone Day. The day we put our plan into action."

"Tomorrow?!" both Poggles gasped. They suddenly realised that all the enjoyable planning and rehearsals had been leading up to this moment.

"Yes – there's no time to waste… The Drones have finished the ray."

If there was one thing Mr and Mrs Sludgebucket could be sure of, it was that they wouldn't see their son before ten o'clock on a Saturday morning. It was hard enough to rouse him on a school day, so they kindly let him lie in at weekends. So it was that Mr Sludgebucket nearly choked on his breakfast when Ernie flew out of his bedpod at nine o'clock and, with a garbled "Bye-I'm-off-to-see-Norman-back-later," slammed the front door behind him.

"But… but… he hasn't even eaten his Wartflakes!" exclaimed Mrs Sludgebucket, dropping her spoon in shock.

Norm and Spong were already waiting at the Zube Tube entrance having just left Mr and Mrs Snodgrass in a similar bemused state. The familiar journey to Professor Zube's laboratory was a quiet one. Both friends anxiously thought about their part in the dangerous plan. Sensing the tension, Spong sat still at Norm's feet, his fur a pale orange.

Shush. The doors of the Zube Tube opened at the Wasteland exit, breaking the silence.

"Well, here goes," Norm laughed uneasily as he led the way.

In his laboratory, Professor Zube greeted the two Poggles cheerily as usual. "Good to see you! I hope you both got a good night's sleep? Busy day today..." he tailed off, and his smile wavered for a fraction of a second. "Right – I suggest we run through the whole plan again and get some final practice in with the radios and mirrors."

The Poggles nodded and obediently collected their equipment from the bench where it had been abandoned the day before. They slipped into the carefully rehearsed routine of movements and commands. Soon they were absorbed in their work.

Both were shocked when, what seemed like only a few moments later, Professor Zube quietly announced, "I think we're ready... It's ten to twelve. Time to get into position."

With those words, the false sense of calm deserted poor Norman. He felt sick to his over-large stomach and wished he'd taken time to eat something for breakfast. His legs felt like jelly but were no match for his feet, which had turned into lumps of clay and wouldn't budge.

"Come on, Norm." Professor Zube gently propelled him out of the laboratory and into the daylight. As they reached the Zube Tube entrance he continued, "So, Ernie, you head back to the Light Side; I'll be just beyond the Waste Dome; and Norm, you'll be on the Dark Side waiting for my signal..." He gently pushed Norm into the Zube Tube entrance. Spong followed.

"It's no good... I can't do it!" Norm blurted. "I'm so sorry, but I really can't!"

"Yep, I was kind of expecting this," Ern said quietly. He lifted a nearby rock and nudged a disgruntled Scudder towards the Zube Tube. "Sorry, Norm, got to be cruel to be kind."

There was muffled scream followed by a familiar *shush* as the Tube whooshed into life.

He's never going to forgive me for that, thought Ernie.

*"Sorry, Norm,
got to be cruel to be kind."*

But on the Dark Side, Norman had already forgotten the Scudder. He was surrounded by blackness such as he'd never known before. Beyond the dim glow of the Zube Tube entrance, there could have been a thousand Scudders. He would never have seen them. If they *were* there, however, they were very, very quiet. The silence was ominous.

Spong pulled softly on his lead to encourage Norman to step into the unknown. Norm's toes began to tingle disconcertingly. He couldn't decide if it was through fear of the dark or something worse. He wiggled them and squinted downwards to try and separate them from the inky blackness. As he stared, something caught his eye. The ring on his toe had begun to glow.

"Norm!" Ernie's voice crackled on the walkie-talkie, making Norman and Spong leap in fright. "I'm so sorry about the Scudder... It was the only way. You understand, don't you?"

"S'alright, Ern. I forgive you. It's good to hear your voice."

"What's it like there?"

"Dark."

"Sorry, daft question. Anything going on?"

"Well, my toes are tingling horribly and my toe-ring has started to glow. What do you think that means?"

"No idea, but it can't be good."

"It's not." The voice of Professor Zube now resonated through the darkness. "We've got to move fast. Ernie, are you in position?"

"Roger."

"Norm, where are you? You need to be twenty paces away from the Zube Tube entrance, remember? Did you count?"

"Sorry, Professor... I got distracted by my toes. I'm not sure how far away I am. Hang on a minute... Spong's pulling on the lead."

"Ha! Good little chap! That's it," the Professor chuckled. "He knows this plan as well as any of us. Just follow him."

A few seconds later Norm announced, "Right, I must be in position, we've stopped."

"OK," said the Professor, "everyone ready? On my count, position your mirrors... THREE... TWO... ONE... NOW!"

An awesome flash of light pierced the darkness, searing Norm's now sensitive eyes. For a moment he was blinded and didn't see a startled rock roll behind him in fright. Norm stumbled and fell backwards, clutching his mirror. As he lay on the ground, the intense shaft of light illuminated the bleak landscape. He looked upwards to where he'd been instructed to reflect the beam and gasped. The measly ping-pong ball model in Professor Zube's laboratory hadn't prepared him for this.

The Dark Planet, home of the Drones, hung low in the sky, pulsating slowly. It seemed close enough to touch, and a chilling air of hopeless misery seeped from it. As his eyes focused, Norm saw with dread that there was movement on its surface. A menacing contraption was pointing directly at him – the UV ray.

The sight of this spurred Norm into action. He scrambled to his feet and angled his mirror to capture Professor Zube's reflected light beam again. He fumbled with his protractor... Any second now he would blast the Dark Planet with light.

"Here we go, Spong! Three... two... WHAT?!"

Everything went black.

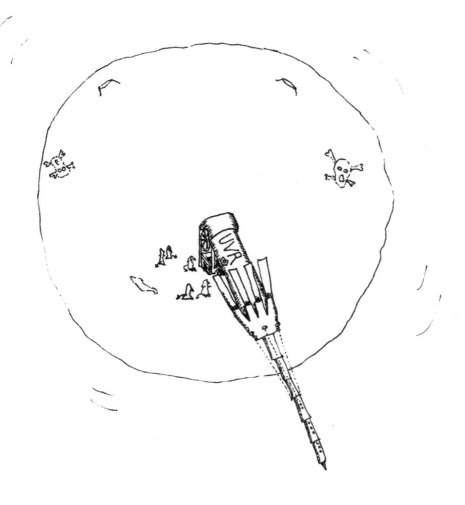

"A menacing contraption was pointing directly at him."

THE LANDING PARTY

"**EVERYTHING'S GONE BLACK, PROFESSOR!**" The voice over the walkie-talkie was Ernie's, not Norman's. "Professor – the Dog Star... it's gone!"

Ernie looked around in dismay. The Light Side of the Green Planet had been plunged into darkness. Groups of frightened Poggles were beginning to gather on the surface, pointing and shouting at the sky. Never in their lifetimes had they seen such a thing.

"Professor! What's happening? What about the plan?" On the Dark Side, Norman felt the panic rise inside him. The ache in his toes was unbearable.

It was several moments before the Professor replied. "I've been a fool," was all he said.

"Tell us what's happening! Is it the Drones?" Now Ernie was panicking too as he found himself being jostled by the growing crowds, running this way and that.

"No. It's an eclipse."

"What does *that* mean?" Ernie felt himself becoming angry at the Professor's lack of explanation. "If you know what's going on, you'd better tell us – things are getting out of hand here!"

"I'm sorry, Poggles, you're right. I'm just cross with myself. I should have realised the timing. I allowed myself to become distracted. What you're seeing is called an eclipse – it happens every now and then when something moves in front of the Dog Star and blocks its light from us. I'd forgotten that Planet Cattus was due to cross its path today. The Drones must have known. That's why they picked this moment to make their move."

"So, it's not forever, then? The light will come back? Ow! Watch where you're going!" Ernie scrambled out of the crater into which he'd been sent flying.

"Yes. Cattus will clear its path shortly and things will be normal again. You'd better tell the nearest Poggle Warden. Get them to calm everyone down."

"OK. I'll try. I don't think it's going to be normal here for a while, though."

A nearby group of Poggles were now lying on the ground, kicking their legs in the air and hooting with their eyes closed. Ernie had no idea how that was supposed to help.

"Perhaps I'd better come over there and explain." The Professor sounded strangely defeated.

"No! You can't! How do you think Poggles will react to the sight of a giant suddenly turning up in the middle of this chaos? It really will send them mad. Anyway, we've still got to finish the plan when the eclipse is over. We've got to stop the Drones, remember?" Why was the Professor being so stupid? Ernie would never normally have to tell him what to do.

"I'm not sure there's much point…"

Ernie was really alarmed now. He'd never heard the Professor be anything other than optimistic. "What are you saying? Of course there's a point – we've got to save the Planet!"

"Ernie, you don't understand. The Drones aren't the only problem. They may as well invade us because the Planet is dying anyway. It's being poisoned."

"A group of Poggles were lying on the ground, kicking their legs in the air and hooting with their eyes closed."

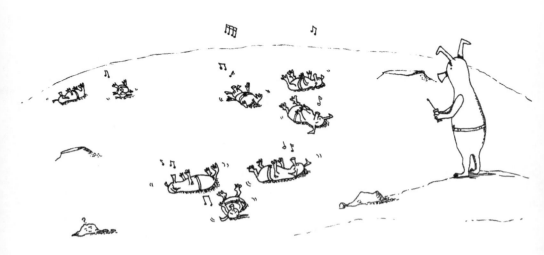

"*What?*" Both walkie-talkies crackled into life.

"I should have told you earlier… I was going to the first time we met, but Norman's toes distracted me. The Elders and I have known for years that something needed to be done. It's our waste – we're running out of space to store it. That's why I 'disappeared' to the Wasteland. I've been monitoring the Waste Dome, collecting samples, reporting back, trying to find a solution – but nothing's worked. The Baracs Beetles used to get rid of it all, but since they died out it just mounts up and becomes toxic. The Dome is nearly full and, if my calculations are right, it won't be long before it explodes… then it's the end for us all."

On the Light Side of the Planet, Ernie watched a sliver of light appear in the sky as the face of the Dog Star peeped out from behind Cattus's shadow once more. A massive cheer erupted from the crowd, but Ernie had never felt so sad.

On the Dark Side of the Planet Norm's pain had numbed him. He couldn't comprehend the enormity of the Professor's words. Spong trembled beside him, and he scooped him up in his arms.

"S'alright, Spong. We'll be OK," he lied.

In the faint light from his toe-ring he saw Spong's fur turn red. Norman was puzzled. White was for fear… red was a warning.

"What's up, Spong?" he whispered, having completely forgotten the Dark Planet above his head. A low buzzing began.

Norman turned slowly and saw a long purple beam descending from the Dark Planet. The beam wasn't made of light as such, but his now accustomed eyes could easily make it out from the thick blackness. And then – something else. Eerie shapes were travelling down the beam… two… four…

five in all. Hooded, dark shapes, moving with slow purpose towards his Planet.

"Professor," he whispered, "they're coming."

"How many?" the Professor replied, far too loudly.

"Five."

"Ah… a Landing Party. They'll do an advance sweep before the main colony descends. You must leave *right now*, Norman."

But Norman couldn't move. The horror in front of him entranced him. The Landing Party reached the surface and, alerted by Professor Zube's voice, five evil, hooded shapes turned towards the sound. Their red eyes bored through the darkness above hooked, beak-like mouths. Behind them, their tails – (*'watch out for their tails!'*) – striped and writhing like separate entities. Now closer, they had seen him, and without any visible signal they began to hum.

Norm's toes trembled in agony. His toe-ring shone, urging him to move, but fear pinned him to the spot. The pitch of the hum rose as the Drones searched for his unique weak point, just as they had done to his ancestors years before.

"Norm, what's that noise?"

The sound of Ernie's voice through the walkie-talkie brought him to his senses and he ran. He was only twenty paces away from the Zube Tube and safety, but twenty paces in the solid blackness might just as well have been a thousand.

The awful hum behind him grew louder, rising in pitch again. Norm's whole body began to shake. He couldn't run anymore. He knew the Drones were close to breaking him and there was nothing he could do but give himself up.

Norman clutched Spong protectively and hung his head. As he stared down and waited for the inevitable, he felt all his pain lift and was afraid no more. The humming reached a crescendo but sounded almost beautiful now as it resonated through him. Then a strange thing happened. His toe-ring, which had been glowing steadily, now focused an intense beam of light ahead of him. At its end he saw a shining globe with a wonderfully familiar 'Z' illuminated on it.

"The Zube Tube! Come on, Spong!" He dropped the wriggling creature, and the two fled towards the light.

Behind him, the Drones cringed from the brightness and their humming ceased, but one of the five was determined. Its red gaze fell to its thrashing tail. It gave an imperceptible nod. Silently, the tail detached itself from its host and slithered to his bidding. Free, and fast as a serpent, it soon overtook its prey.

"Silently, the tail detached itself from its host..."

Norm was breathless as he reached the Zube Tube entrance. With relief, he stretched out his hand to push the button that would take him home – but something was in the way. Why was Spong's leash blocking his path? But the lead didn't have stripes *or* thrash of its own accord. Realisation hit him just as the Drone's tail reared like a cobra in front of him. With nothing to lose, Norm leapt over it and punched the brass button on the wall.

Several things happened at once. A furry red blur flew in front of Norman, just as the tail lunged and struck. Norm landed inside the Zube Tube and pulled Spong to safety behind him. The doors slid shut with a 'shush' and the tail reared again, slamming angrily against them. An awful yellow ooze dripped down the glass outside.

In the pause before the Zube whooshed him away, Norm knew something was wrong. The leash in his hand was limp. Spong lay motionless on the floor, yellow venom dripping from a patch of his fur.

"Spong… no!" Norm cried; but as he watched, the tiny creature turned from red to a sickly green.

THE ANTIDOTE

BANG, BANG, BANG!

THE SNODGRASS'S FRONT door nearly rattled off its hinges.

BANG, BANG, BANG!

"Arthur! What on the Planet is it? Is the sky falling in now?" Isadora Snodgrass's voice quavered timidly from the living pod where she was sitting with her feet up, drinking nerve tonic tea. The afternoon had been a trying one, what with the pandemonium caused by the eclipse... and now this.

"Stay put, dear, I'll find out what's going on." Arthur Snodgrass patted his wife's hand and strode into the hall.

"What the...?" he exclaimed as he opened the door. There was his son Norman, bedraggled and terrified, holding... That couldn't be Spong?

"Dad, help me... it's Spong... he's... I don't think he..."

"Come in quickly, Son, we need your mother."

Isadora Snodgrass assessed the situation in an instant, her nerves miraculously healing themselves as she took charge. "What did this?" she asked as she examined her patient. She only paused for a second, drawing in her breath, as she registered Norman's reply.

"A Drone's tail."

"Good heavens!" exclaimed his father. "How did that happen? Where did you see a Drone?"

"Questions later," his mother interrupted firmly. "We must act fast."

For the next few minutes Arthur Snodgrass quietly obeyed his wife's instructions to set a fire and fetch blankets and old towels, while she busied herself in the kitchen. Norm watched in wonder as his mother consulted a tatty old notebook then proceeded to collect various herbs and powders from her store cupboard. She put a pan of hot water on to boil and reached to the back of her collection of teapots.

"There you are," she said as she retrieved a large, black and orange striped pot that Norman had never seen before.

"It was your grandmother's," she replied to his questioning gaze. "Not been used for a very long time."

She blew the dust from its spout and quickly rinsed it. Then, muttering quietly, she began to measure a pinch of this powder, a spoonful of that and a leaf or two from various dusty packets into the striped pot. A musty smell emerged from it as she poured the boiling water on top.

"Ten minutes and the antidote will be ready. I hope we're not too late."

Back in the living pod, Arthur Snodgrass had made a roaring fire and the cosiest of beds. Using old towels and hot water as instructed, he carefully bathed Spong's wound and wiped away as much of the venom as he could. Despite his efforts, Spong was a pitiful sight and shivered uncontrollably as he lay there. Gently, Isadora propped him up and dripped the freshly brewed antidote tea onto his tongue. Spong coughed and spluttered but his eyes remained closed.

"... a pinch of this powder, a spoonful of that..."

"What happens now?" Norm asked hopefully.

"Now we wait," she said. "In the meantime, I want you to drink this. You look awful." She handed him a mug of nerve tonic tea and Norm sipped gratefully.

"You'd better tell us exactly what's been going on."

There are times when only the truth will do, and Norman knew that this was one of those times. Any punishment his parents might bestow upon him was nothing compared to what he had witnessed that day.

And so he began... The disappearance of Spong, the night-time visit to the Wasteland, meeting Professor Zube... patiently he told them all. There were muffled sobs from his mother on hearing the words spoken by Ilona Quinn and about the toe-ring given to her son by the Master Poggle himself. The fire had died to quiet embers by the time Norman told them of the Professor's plan to defeat the Drones. He fought back tears as he related his awful encounter with them that had resulted in dear, faithful Spong being stung while trying to save him.

"Well!" was all his mother could say. His father meanwhile had a curious look on his face – a mixture of concern and... was that pride?

Another loud knock at the door broke the silence and heralded the arrival of Bill and Freda Sludgebucket. Ernie trailed miserably behind them. He gave his friend a weak smile and shot a worried look at Spong.

"Afternoon, Arthur, Izzy. Sorry to trouble you but things have to be said," said Bill, looking anxiously at his wife, who pursed her mouth and nodded for him to continue.

"We know your Norman's normally a good lad, and Ernie thinks the Planet of him, but he's gone too far this time. Led him astray he has and put all sorts of nonsense into his head about giant Professors and monsters on the Dark Side. Poor Ernie can't stop babbling about it. He says the Groans are coming and we've got to do something about it."

"The Drones, you mean, Bill?" Arthur Snodgrass replied calmly.

"What? Don't tell me he's got you at it now. You don't believe all this rubbish, do you? Next you'll be telling us you've invited the giant for tea!"

Freda Sludgebucket tittered at her husband's sarcasm. There was another knock at the door.

"Answer that, please, Norman. Bill, Freda, why don't you sit down. I think a pot of tea is called for." His father steered them firmly to the sofa where they sat down with a bump. Norman returned.

"Better make that a large pot, Mum. Can I introduce you all to Professor Zube?"

Four pairs of eyes gawped at a point above Norman's head as Professor Zube ducked into the room.

"Very pleased to meet you all; Norman and Ernie have told me so much about you. I hope you don't mind me dropping in like this but it is rather urgent."

Arthur Snodgrass was the first to recover himself. "My goodness, Professor! I never thought I'd see the day. You are most welcome indeed. Izzy, don't just stand there; put the kettle on." He shook the Professor's hand warmly and looked round for a suitable chair. On finding none big enough, he placed a pile of cushions on the dining table. Professor Zube sat down graciously. The dining table creaked.

"*Now* do you believe me?" Ernie said triumphantly to his parents who were still agog on the sofa.

Ten minutes later, a pot of refreshing tea had done much to relieve the shock. Mrs Sludgebucket's cup still rattled against her saucer, but now she was smiling up at the Professor as if he were a celebrity.

Isadora had excelled herself, wheeling in a trolley with no less than three teapots: a silver one with gold stars on it for Professor Zube (she poured the entire contents into a vase for him); a plain black one for the main party; and, much to Norman's dismay, *his* tea was once again served in the Fib Pot. Its spout was now so long that his mother had to use a ruler to splint it sufficiently to pour.

"Mrs Snodgrass," began the Professor after draining his vase.

"Oh, call me Izzy, please!"

Norman shot a horrified look at Ernie – was his mother flirting?

"Izzy, I must congratulate you on your brewing proficiency. A very fine blend indeed. But more importantly, the antidote you have prepared for Spong – poor, brave creature," he wiped his eye. "Only time will tell if he... Well, the next twenty-four hours are crucial, but he stands the best chance now, thanks to you."

Isadora Snodgrass blushed.

"Professor Zube, Norman's been telling us about the Drones. Is it right they're back?"

"I'm afraid so... May I call you Arthur? Yes, they've returned to the Dark Side despite your son's heroic efforts today. Just a Landing Party at the moment. They'll report back to their Planet after they've scouted around – but you know what follows. Did Norman tell you about the toxic waste?"

Freda Sludgebucket slopped her tea into her saucer.

"I really don't think this is the sort of conversation to be having in front of young Poggles!" she quailed.

"Norman, why don't you take Ernie to your room? He can keep you company while you tidy it." His mother's tone was non-negotiable. Norman shot a protesting look at the Professor.

"Perhaps that's a good idea, Norman; it will give me a chance to talk to your parents."

Arthur Snodgrass shut the living pod door firmly behind them. "How bad is it?"

"I won't lie to you. We have a serious problem. I've been in the Wasteland for years now trying to come up with the answer. It's not just the *amount* of waste we produce but the fact that over time it ferments and produces toxic gases. You should see the Waste Dome – it could explode at any moment."

"Does Zohar know?" Bill Sludgebucket asked.

"Oh, absolutely. He foresaw the problem years ago when the Baracs Beetles disappeared. He knew they were the only thing controlling the waste. He asked me to move to the Wasteland and keep him up to date with the smallest detail – I speak to him every day." There was an awed gasp at this.

"I've tried everything I can think of but nothing works. The thing is, I'm to blame for the whole problem. If I hadn't introduced the waste-pipe system, the Baracs Beetles wouldn't have died out in the first place. It's too late now – too much of the stuff has built up – an *army* of beetles would never get rid of it all."

"There must be something we can do." Arthur Snodgrass leaned forward. "Every problem has a solution. Let me tell you what I did with the brooms at work. The handles kept coming out and—"

"Not now, dear," his wife interjected.

"Right, well, I'm just saying there's got to be a way."

"I'm certainly open to any ideas you have, Arthur; two heads are always better than one. We don't have much time, though."

Norman was fuming as he paced the length of his bedpod.

"So it's OK for me to face a bunch of Drones single-handed on the Dark Side, but I'm not allowed to be in the same room while they talk about dung!"

He dragged the vacuum cleaner angrily behind him. (This had also been introduced to the Planet by the Professor and was very efficient at cleaning up space dust.)

"Sorry, Norm, it's my mum's fault. Just because I'm the youngest she treats me like I'm her baby. She went loopy when I told her what had been going on. Now she's just trying to pretend nothing's happened. As if *that's* going to make a difference."

Norman continued to pace.

"What were they like?" Ernie asked hesitantly.

Norman stopped. "The worst thing I've ever seen. And when they look at you…" He paced again to shake the image from his mind.

"Is this really *it*, then?"

"I don't know – it doesn't seem real. To think, two days ago I was worried about homework!" The friends laughed in spite of everything.

"Well, if the Planet's going to end, you may as well face it with a tidy bedpod. Are you actually going to plug that thing in?!"

Norman looked at the flex trailing uselessly behind him. He'd been so preoccupied he hadn't realised it wasn't connected. He plugged it in and reached to flick the switch on the machine.

WHOOMPF!

The whole room filled with dust.

Seconds later, two sets of parents and a Professor crammed into the bedpod doorway to see Norman and Ernie choking and blinking in the dust.

"What have you done!?" shouted Mrs Snodgrass.

"I'm sorry, Mum. I wasn't concentrating. I turned it on to blow instead of suck. I don't think it's been emptied in a while…" But before his mother could scold him further, a triumphant cry came from Professor Zube.

"I don't believe it! That's the answer! You fantastic Poggle – you've just saved the Planet!"

Whoompf!
"The whole room filled with dust."

THE SWITCH

THE LIVING POD WAS A MESS.

Teacups, papers and pencils were strewn across the dining table and spilled onto the floor. Everyone was talking at the same time, gesticulating excitedly and occasionally pausing to scribble on fresh sheets of paper. A thin film of dust from the exploded vacuum had wafted through from Norm's bedpod and was whirling around in the flurry of activity.

Disturbed by the eruption, Scheherazade crept out from her hiding place. Upon seeing the wonderful mess of dirt, she felt as if all her birthdays had come at once. *Definitely worth exploring,* she thought.

The hullaballoo in the living pod sounded interesting, though – perhaps there was a good story to overhear first? Keeping to the shadows, she pattered across the hall and scooted under the sofa. There she sat, chewing a tasty morsel of dust and listening intently.

"I think it could work, Professor!" Arthur Snodgrass shook the Professor's hand vigorously. His mechanical mind had been the first to grasp the brilliant simplicity of the idea. "We'll turn the Zube Tube into a giant hoover!"

"That's it, Arthur! If we connect the pipes feeding the Waste Dome to the Zube Tube network and literally switch the mechanism from suck to blow – just as clever Norman showed us – we'll blast the Dark Planet into space and kill two birds with one stone. No more Drones and no more toxic waste – it's sheer genius!"

"Wait a minute, you didn't say anything about killing birds – whatever *they* are. I'm not having anything to do with that!" Freda Sludgebucket protested.

"No, no, dear lady, we won't be killing birds, or anything else for that matter – it's a figure of speech, you understand."

She didn't, but warily held her tongue.

"Of course, we'll need a pipe to direct the flow on the Dark Side," continued the Professor. "Just like the hoover, really. Otherwise the muck will just splurge all over the ground."

"I can see a problem there." Arthur Snodgrass scratched his head. "It'll have to be a pretty big pipe, and the force of all the gunge inside will make it very difficult to control. It'll be wobbling all over the place."

There was quiet in the room as everyone pondered the problem. The clock ticked loudly. Sherri stopped chewing, her eight eyes glittering.

"I know," Isadora Snodgrass picked up the Fib Pot, "we can splint it."

The Professor eyed the Fib Pot's spout, now held rigidly by the wooden ruler and tape.

"A veritable family of masterminds!" he clapped. "That's perfect. We'll aim the pipe at the Dark Planet and prop it up in place. I'm sure we can find a way of doing that."

Arthur Snodgrass winked at Bill Sludgebucket.

"Well, you don't work down a sugar mine all your life without learning a thing or two about supporting tunnels. What do you say we borrow some pit props from the mine tonight, Bill? I'm sure the boss won't mind – under the circumstances!"

"Sounds reasonable," Bill replied with a chuckle. "I'll give you a hand."

Norm and Ernie exchanged impressed glances. They'd never seen their parents as animated, and after the events of the last few days they were very happy to let them take charge. Norm put another log on the fire and stroked Spong. He still felt cold to the touch.

The Professor added some diagrams to the sheet nearest him, talking as he went. "It's really coming together now – a few tweaks and I think we're there. It will be simple enough to connect the two networks… We just need to cut a hole through and seal it well. Then I'll need to set the flaps on the Zube network so we don't get any blow-back through the system."

"That would be most unpleasant." Freda Sludgebucket raised her eyebrows. "Izzy, I think Poggles need to be warned not to use the Zube at the same time."

"Good idea, Freda. Professor, perhaps the Master Poggle could notify the Poggle Wardens? They could put notes through everyone's doors."

"Yes, you're probably right. The old tubes are a bit cranky these days; better safe than sorry. I'll have a chat with Zohar tonight."

"Close your mouth, Freda," Bill Sludgebucket whispered to his wife, who was astounded to hear the Professor refer so casually to their Master.

"He speaks to him *every day*," Isadora reminded her friend. "And do you see that toe-ring our Norman's wearing? Gift from Zohar himself!" Freda gawped again.

"Now, the switch will need to be positioned by the Zube Tube on the Dark Side. Norman, I'm afraid you'll have to be the one to throw it when the time comes. Your long toes will warn you well in advance if there is any danger."

Norman nodded quietly; it was just as he'd expected.

"Wait a minute, you're not sending him back there! I forbid it!" Isadora Snodgrass looked to her husband for support.

Arthur Snodgrass put his arm around her shoulders.

"Izzy, you know I think the Planet of our Norman... and if I could change any of this I would. The fact is, we knew this day would probably come, didn't we? He's a Long-Toed Poggle. We can't ignore it – this is what he was born to do..."

"It's true, Mum. There's no need to worry, though; we'll wait till the Landing Party of Drones has gone, won't we, Professor?"

"Oh, absolutely. I'll make certain of that. Then it will just be a matter of attaching the pipe at the Zube entrance, propping it up and flicking the switch. What could possibly go wrong?"

Norman laughed weakly. He was secretly thinking that there was a lot of scope for him to muck things up completely, as usual.

"Right, we'd better get on with it. If you round up those pit props tonight, I'll pop over to Zohar and let him know the plan. What say we all meet at my Laboratory in the morning? I think you'll like what I've done with it, Arthur."

"I'd be delighted, Professor! Norman and Ernie can show me the way." Arthur Snodgrass nodded enthusiastically.

"Oh no. You might be happy for *Norman* to risk his life but Ernie's not having any part in this." Freda Sludgebucket had found her voice once more. "*He* hasn't got any special toes to protect him; and besides, he needs to stay home and practise his hooting."

Ernie looked at his mother aghast. How could she worry about hooting when the entire Planet's future hung in the balance?

"Actually, Mrs Sludgebucket, Ernie's a critical part of the plan – isn't that right, Professor?" Norman looked pointedly at Professor Zube.

"What? Oh, yes, yes indeed – crucial member of the team; we can't do without him. You must be very proud to have such a son, my dear Freda!"

Freda Sludgebucket's eyes narrowed for a moment but then she blushed.

"Well… if you put it like that, I suppose he'd better go along. Not that I'm surprised you can't do without him. He's always been the brainy one in our family. I think he gets it from me…" Bill Sludgebucket choked on his mouthful of tea.

"Thanks, Norm!" Ernie whispered as his mother chattered away happily.

Later that evening, a small group of Poggles gathered outside the office pod of Wilbur Faircop, Chief Poggle Warden, and watched him pin a notice to his door.

"No need to crowd! You'll all be getting one of these through your letterboxes tonight. Special orders from the Master Poggle himself."

"What does it say?" An elderly Poggle with very thick glasses strained to read from the back of the huddle.

"It says that all Poggles should refrain from using the Zube Tubes tomorrow, and until further notice, for health and safety reasons. There's some essential maintenance being carried out on the section near the Wasteland."

"That's stupid," Boris Whinge mumbled under his breath. "I don't see why the whole network has to be out of bounds. Hey, Jeli, we can have great fun whizzing around on them with no one else about! What do you think?"

Jeli Mould sighed, "Why do we *always* have to do the exact opposite of what we're asked? Maybe for once there's a good reason?"

"What's the matter, Jeli? Not losing your bottle, are you? Or maybe you're afraid of getting into trouble in case your boyfriend Norman finds out? You're turning into a nerd like him."

"Oh, why don't you just shut up!" And with that, Jeli stormed off, leaving an astounded Boris in her wake.

Back at the Snodgrass residence, all had finally fallen quiet. More dust had settled on the abandoned papers and cups which, unusually, hadn't been tidied away. The day's events had been exhausting, and three weary Poggles now lay snoring in their bedpods.

Only one creature stirred. The beady eyes of Scheherazade the Scudder blinked in the darkness. Quietly, she crept out from under the sofa and climbed the leg of the dining table.

Most interesting… she thought to herself as she studied the plans scattered across it. A whimper broke the silence. Deep in his wretched sleep, Spong was re-living the attack of the Drone's tail.

Softly, Scheherazade descended and made her way over to his basket. Settling herself next to Spong she softly wove a tale of wondrous bravery into his ear, and there she stayed all night, keeping watch over her charge.

"… keeping watch over her charge."

FALL AND RISE

"**WELL, I NEVER!**" Arthur Snodgrass exclaimed.

"Isn't it incredible, Dad? Just like I said!"

The pleasure of showing his father around Professor Zube's Laboratory erased the memory of their emotional send-off moments earlier.

Norman's mother had given him a hug, so fierce it squeezed the breath out of him. She'd then hurried back into the pod without looking over her shoulder, saying she didn't have time for this nonsense when there was fresh antidote tea to make. Her tearful sniffs could be heard from the kitchen however.

Poor Ernie hadn't got off so lightly. He still had the red lipstick marks from his mother's many kisses plastered on his face.

"What wouldn't I give for a space like this...?" Norman's father whistled with admiration as he studied the fantastic array of books and experiments competing for attention.

"I knew you'd appreciate it." The Professor smiled proudly. "I recognise a kindred spirit in you – a fellow enquiring mind, eh? In fact, when this is all over, it would be my absolute pleasure if you were to become a regular visitor. I could clear a workbench for you if you like?"

Arthur Snodgrass was gobsmacked. He shook the Professor's hand warmly and his eyes shone.

"That's settled, then. We'd best get on. There's been a bit of activity on the surface of the Dark Planet this morning. I wouldn't mind betting they're preparing to welcome the Landing Party back. We need to get cracking."

"Righto, Professor; the boys and I can finalise the hoover-pipe-what's-his-name, if you want to see about connecting the waste pipes to the Zube? We've brought some supplies from the sugar mine that should do the trick."

For the next two hours, the three Poggles worked in harmony. Through years of helping his father, Norman was able to anticipate his every move. He knew which tool was needed and when, and was ready with a hammer, screwdriver or pliers before he could be asked. Ernie soon slotted into the team, lifting bits of wood, or holding a jar of Firelighters up to help Mr Snodgrass see.

Before long, the trio had completed their task, and a giant flexible hose stood in the Laboratory supported at either end by criss-crossed pit props.

"All you've got to do, Norman," his father explained, "is attach one end to the Zube Tube entrance with this thick tape. Then move the other end so it's pointing... Well, you know where. When you're ready, unscrew the button marked 'To the Wasteland' from the Zube Tube control panel. Then replace it with this reverse switch." He handed Norm a small brass knob.

"How will I move it into place on my own, Dad? It takes two of us to lift one of those props as it is."

"Not a problem," his father grinned, and reached into his tool-bag; "only don't tell your mother. These are the casters from her tea trolley!" He pulled out four wheels and deftly attached them to the bottom of the pit props. The pipe now glided smoothly with just the push of a finger.

"Mum'll go off her trolley too when she discovers they're missing!" Norman was delightfully shocked at his dad's resourcefulness.

"Let me worry about that; you've got enough on your plate," his father grinned.

"I wonder how the Professor's getting on outside," Ernie said anxiously.

"Here he comes now; you can ask him," said Norm.

The green button by the airlock lit up and the Professor emerged waving a telescope. "Action stations!" he exclaimed, rushing over to them. "I've just seen the Landing Party return to the Dark Planet. We've only got a small window of time."

"We are mobile, sir!" Norman's father unwittingly saluted the Professor as he demonstrated the newly wheeled contraption.

"Excellent work!" The Professor clapped them all on the shoulders. "And I've connected the two networks successfully so we're all systems go – or rather, all systems blow! Hee-hee!"

Despite the awfulness of the joke, Norman found himself laughing. "I'm ready, Professor," he said, "and I won't need a Scudder this time, Ern."

"Of course you won't," Professor Zube agreed. "There's no danger. The Drones are back on their Planet for now. It's just a question of fixing the pipe, flicking the switch and then back home for a nice cup of tea. Mind you, you'll have to walk back through the old tunnels as the Zube will be out of action after the blast. I've got the TWITs and SPANNERS on standby for the clean-up operation but it'll take a while."

Norman allowed himself a moment to imagine his favourite tea back home, which his mother had promised him. He could almost taste the Green Bug butter sandwiches. "Let's do it," he said, flicking the brass switch into the air with uncharacteristic bravado and astonishing his audience by catching it in the same hand.

Norman's confidence was short-lived. As he pulled the giant pipe out of the Zube Tube on the Dark Side, the solid blackness engulfed him once more. He'd forgotten how lonely it was there, and his toes ached with the memory of his last visit.

"Snap out of it, Norm," he told himself, "you've got a job to do."

The pipe was not as easy to manoeuvre on the rough surface of the Planet and it took several moments of pushing to get it into place. Eventually, though, it co-operated, and Norm forced himself to look up at the Dark Planet, visible only as a denser shade of blackness above him. He shuddered and thought of its gruesome occupants as he aimed the tube towards them.

Ooh, my toes are really aching now, he thought. *This toe-ring must be super sensitive if it picks them up from that far away.* He wriggled them to ease the cramping. *The sooner I throw the switch the better.*

He felt his way back to the Zube Tube entrance by following the pipe, and began taping the end. Despite his urge to hurry, he made himself work slowly and carefully. By the time he had finished, there was a secure 'waste-tight' seal with the Zube Tube and only a few centimetres of tape remained on the reel.

Dad would be proud, he thought. *Now to fix the switch.*

Norman retrieved the small brass knob from the bag hanging on his belt. He began unscrewing the 'Wasteland' button on the control panel as instructed but, whether through nerves or haste, it was no easy task. The small button was fiddly and kept sticking on its thread. Norman had to stretch to reach it, which made the cramp in his toes worse, and by the time he'd worked it loose he was quite cross. He quickly screwed the brass reverse switch into place and gave it an angry wrench to tighten it.

PLINK.

The tiny metal knob snapped off in his hand and dropped to the floor. Norman went cold with shock. He grabbed the walkie-talkie from its loop on his belt.

"Professor... Professor... can you hear me?"

"Loud and clear, Norman, how's it going? Are you ready to throw the switch?"

"No... I've broken it. I'm so sorry... What shall I do?"

"Oh dear... Well, don't worry. Give me a second and I'll think of something..."

"Please hurry; it's so dark here and my toes are really hurting again."

"Don't panic, Norman, you're quite safe; the Landing Party has gone, remember?"

"Are you sure, Professor? I feel really weird."

"Absolutely. I saw all four Drones beam back up."

"But Professor…"

"What is it, Norman?"

"There were five…"

As Norman held the walkie-talkie up to his face, he saw two red eyes reflected on its plastic screen. There was no need to look behind – he simply ran for his life. Stumbling through the blackness, he knew the Drone was following, but there was nowhere to hide. What was he to do?

Stupidly, he found himself thinking with annoyance that he would miss his favourite tea. His mother would be preparing it for him now… She hated food going to waste. Norman felt a lump rise in his throat at the thought of her. He ran with all his might.

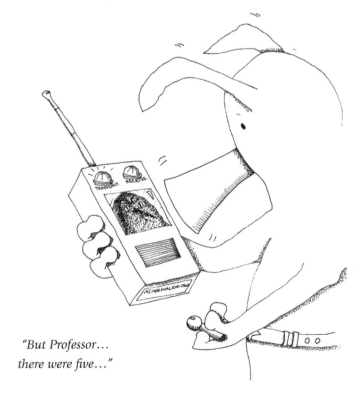

*"But Professor…
there were five…"*

Suddenly, his foot jerked to the right. Still running, Norman looked down – the toe-ring was glowing again and… yes, it was trying to pull his foot! Without questioning, he obeyed its command and changed direction. He had no idea where he was or how far he'd travelled – he could be going round in circles for all he knew – but something told him to follow the ring and it would lead him to safety.

CRASH!

Norman flew through the air and landed with a bump on something cold and flat that had tripped him up. Winded for a moment, he lay dazed on the ground and felt the object. It was his mirror! He must have dropped it there when the Landing Party had chased him.

Quickly, Norman scrambled to his feet and hauled it upright. He heard a noise to his left and spun round just in time to thrust the mirror between him and the full horror of the Drone. Its beak almost touched the glass. Its two red eyes narrowed, and it sniffed. It was so close, Norman could feel its breath on his hands and smell its awful rotting skin.

The Drone considered its dim reflection… It had never seen itself before. It twisted its hooded head from side to side. It was puzzled. From the corner of his eye, Norman saw its tail flick round the side of the mirror. The tail stopped still, almost as if it had seen him and was pondering what to do. Then it reared up…

Without thinking, Norman pushed his full weight against the mirror, throwing the startled Drone backwards.

Thinking it had been attacked by its own reflection, it let out a howl of surprise. As it struggled to its feet, surprise turned to rage as it saw the Poggle in front of it. Norman waited for its awful tail to strike again; but before the Drone could retaliate, a beam of light hit it squarely in the face. The Drone recoiled in terror, shielding its eyes with its claws, then with a shriek of frustration the hideous creature fled into the darkness.

Norman turned to see where the light had come from. Two dark figures were approaching and one seemed to have a bright eye in the centre of its head. Seconds later, Norman collapsed with relief into the arms of his father and Ernie.

"Blimey, Norm! Was that a...?"

Norman nodded weakly. His father lifted him to his feet.

"We thought you might like some company for the walk home," he said. "The Professor lent me his miner's headlamp to guide us. I didn't think I'd be scaring off a Drone with it! Are you alright? What was he up to?"

"There's no time to explain. I haven't thrown the switch yet – it broke off in my hand and... Oh Dad, what if that Drone's gone to raise the alarm? It will all be over..."

Norman's father frowned.

"The show's not over till the fat Poggle hoots," he said, striding off to the Zube Tube entrance, which to Norman's amazement was only a few feet away.

"Hmm... you did a good job of the seal, Norm, couldn't have done better myself. Unfortunately, you also did a good job of snapping the switch. Sheared it right off at the base." He chuntered away to himself as he unclipped a small tool-bag from his utility belt.

"Good thing I brought my fine-nosed pliers and some old wire." He set to repairing the switch.

"Er... Mr Snodgrass?" Ernie sounded anxious.

"Hang on a minute, Ernie, I need to concentrate."

"But Mr Snodgrass... something's happening in the sky."

Arthur Snodgrass paused, still gripping a piece of wire between his teeth.

"Great heavens!" he said.

Norman had been right. The fleeing Drone had indeed raised the alarm and the Dark Planet was once more bathed in ultraviolet light. The whole surface of it appeared to be moving as rank upon rank of Drones marched slowly in one purposeful direction.

"The UV ray!" blurted Ernie. "Is that it?"

Norman nodded.

"Any minute now, they'll travel down it."

"Not if we've got anything to do with it..." His Father gritted his teeth and continued furiously twisting wire to create a makeshift switch.

Above them, a shaft of ultraviolet light began to form and stretch towards them as the UV ray throbbed into life once more.

"Mr Snodgrass – they're coming!" Ernie needlessly pointed to a throng of hooded shapes descending slowly down the beam.

Arthur Snodgrass gave a final twist of his pliers then spoke to his son. "Now, Norman! Throw the switch!"

Norman didn't need telling twice.

KAA-
BOOOM!

The entire contents of the Waste Dome spewed into the air with the force of a hundred meteorites.

Like a giant marble in a playground, the stinking mass hit the Dark Planet and sent it spinning away into the Universe. Those Drones which had begun beaming down found themselves whirling aimlessly in space instead, their furious cries doomed to go unheard forever.

On the Dark Side of the Green Planet, three Poggles picked themselves up from the ground where they'd been thrown by the force of the blast.

"Who fancies a nice cup of tea?" said Arthur Snodgrass, dusting himself down.

Without waiting for a reply, he adjusted the lamp on his head, put an arm round Norman and Ernie and guided them towards the tunnel that would take them home.

"Kaa-booom!"

BOY MEETS GIRL

THE SHOCK OF his ordeal caught up with Norman as they trudged back home. His knees wobbled and a puff of wind would have toppled him.

He was grateful to have his father and best friend to lean on but, as they finally reached home, something far more tangible knocked him over. The front door burst open and an orange blur flew down the path and threw itself at him.

"Spong!" Norman cried in delight, trying to fend off the frenzy of licks and squeaks whilst flat on his back. "Ernie, he's OK!"

"Yep, I can see that!" Ernie laughed, retrieving the now yellow ball from Norman's face and giving it an affectionate ruffle.

Norm regained his feet only to be winded again, this time by his mother, whose hug, if it were possible, was tighter than ever.

"Everyone's here and tea's ready, so hurry up and wash your hands," she said, just as if he'd come home from a normal day at school. Only the slightest quaver in her voice betrayed her relief.

His mother was right – everyone was indeed there. Alerted by Ernie on the walkie-talkie, Professor Zube had hurried to give Mrs Snodgrass the news that all were safe and well. She in turn had rallied the Sludgebuckets, and the whole ensemble was once more crammed into the living pod.

The dining table groaned under a sumptuous buffet tea that would have done the Master Poggle himself proud. There were three types of Boulder Buns, Fairy Cakes sprinkled with space dust, piles of Green Bug butter sandwiches, a jug of Beetle Juice and, of course, a large pot of tea in the silver starred pot.

A colossal cheer erupted as Norman entered the room, and he found himself being slapped on the back, hugged and squeezed from all angles. Mouths were opening and closing all around but Norman couldn't make out any words in the bedlam.

"Give him some room! Give him some room!" his mother intervened, recognising that he was completely dazed. She steered him to an armchair and thrust a cup of hot sweet tea into his hand. "Drink this," she ordered. "You two as well…" She poured two more cups, for Ernie and his father.

As he drank the warming brew, Norman felt his strength return. Spong jumped onto his lap, made a few circuits to find the comfiest place and curled up into a contented ball.

"When did he recover?" Norm asked, rubbing Spong's favourite sweet spot behind his ear.

"About half an hour after you left this morning," his mother replied. "The second batch of antidote did the trick. He's been up and down the hallway waiting for you since then – that is, when he's not been squeaking at something under your bed. I don't know what you've got in there but he's certainly fascinated by it."

"Let's hope it's not a Scudder!" chuckled Ernie.

"Don't even joke about it!" Norm looked nervously around.

"Are you telling me you'll happily fight off a Drone but you're still afraid of Scudders?" his father asked incredulously.

"Fight off a Drone?! What was he doing fighting off a Drone?" Isadora Snodgrass was horrified.

"Er... well," Arthur Snodgrass faltered, realising he'd put his three-toed foot in it.

"I'm afraid it's all my fault, Isadora." Professor Zube looked mortified as he explained his error in counting the Landing Party. "I would never have sent Norman to the Dark Side if I'd known... I was certain they'd all returned."

"All's well that ends well, Professor. And anyway, that Drone was no match for our Norm," said Arthur.

The Professor smiled gratefully. "Are you ready to tell us what happened?" he asked gently.

Norman took another mouthful of tea, gazed around at the expectant faces in the room and nodded.

For several minutes all was still, as Norman relayed what had taken place on the Dark Side. Everyone held their breath when he reached the moment that he realised the Drone was behind him. They gasped as he described how his toe-ring had directed his feet. Norman himself felt detached, as if he were floating above his own body watching someone else tell the story. Had all this really happened to him?

Ernie and his father picked up the tale from the point where they'd emerged from the tunnel into the pitch black.

"We had no idea where you were but then we heard this crash," Ernie began.

"Yes, that must have been when you pushed the Drone over with your mirror," his father continued. "I looked over to where the noise was coming from and got the shock of my life to see the darned thing there!"

"Not as big as the shock those Drones got when you blasted them, eh Norm! KAAA-BOOOOOOMMMM!!!!" Ernie rolled on the floor, re-enacting Drones whirling into space, causing Spong to jump down and run around him in circles.

Mrs Snodgrass held up her hands. "I think we've all had quite enough excitement for one day. Tea won't eat itself, and I've no doubt you're all hungry. Help yourselves!"

Norman suddenly realised he was famished. He reached for the plate of his favourite Green Bug butter sandwiches but before he could tuck in, something in the hallway caught his eye.

Zohar, Master Poggle, stepped into the room. Everyone froze, mouths mid-chew, teacups aloft and eyes astonished, unable to comprehend the great presence in the room.

"Forgive me interrupting like this, Poggles – I did knock but there was no reply and the door was open…"

Still no one spoke. Thankfully, Professor Zube stepped in to make the introductions. "Good to see you, Zohar! I wasn't sure if you'd got my message." The Professor shook his hand and led him into the room.

"This is Arthur Snodgrass… his wife Isadora… Norman you know, of course… his good friend Ernie Sludgebucket… and Ernie's parents Bill and Freda."

One by one Zohar shook hands with everyone, politely ignoring the confusion and juggling of buns and sandwiches as Poggles tried to bow or curtsey with hands and mouths full.

One creature in the room had no intention of standing on ceremony however, and an excited yellow ball launched itself into Zohar's arms.

"Spong!" cried Norman with embarrassment. "Get down! I'm so sorry, sir – he's very friendly. He doesn't know who he's jumping at."

"On the contrary," Zohar laughed as Spong started licking his face, "he knows very well, don't you, Spong? Good to see you're fully recovered. Yes, yes, I'm pleased to see you too, but down you get. Be good for your Master." He gently lowered Spong to the floor and patted him as he sat obediently by his feet.

"His Master?" Ernie blurted out, forgetting himself. "You mean Spong belongs to *you*, sir?"

"He does indeed, young Ernie. Spong has been my faithful companion for a very long time."

"Then why did Miss Lastic say he was the new school pet, sir…? And why did she choose me to look after him?" Norman had always thought that was strange.

"I'm afraid you've been rather set up, Norman." Professor Zube smiled. "As you know, Zohar has been concerned about the future for many years. He knew there were troubled times ahead. He also knew that a certain Long-Toed Poggle was born eight years ago who might play a part in saving the entire Planet. It was only sensible to loan Spong to you to protect you."

"And all the while you thought you were looking after *him*!" Ernie shook his head in disbelief.

Norman was quiet. He knew he should be thanking the Master for his generous kindness but the word 'loan' weighed heavily on his heart. It was slowly dawning on him that he would have to part with Spong – and maybe very soon.

"Oh, Master! How can we ever thank you for your consideration?" Norman's mother remembered her manners despite her shock. "If I'd known you were coming I would have baked a cake!" She looked pointedly at Professor Zube.

"It is I who am indebted to you, dear lady." Zohar bowed graciously towards her. "We have asked an awful lot of your son and he has shown incredible bravery." Turning to Norman, he continued, "I do have one further request of you however…"

Norman nodded, amazed to receive such attention from one so great.

"You have taken such good care of Spong, and he has grown very attached to you since he has been here. Sadly, I find myself slowing up and less able to take him on the long walks he needs. I wonder if you would consider continuing to look after him for me… if your parents wouldn't mind?"

"Would I?!" Norman picked Spong up and hugged him, receiving fresh licks in return.

"Thank you, Norman. I do hope you and Ernie will walk him over to visit me every so often?"

"Yes, sir!" they replied.

"Thank you both. Now, with your permission, I must be on my way – there is much to prepare."

"Ah yes, the anniversary celebrations are the day after tomorrow, aren't they?" said Professor Zube.

"Indeed, but in light of recent events I'm considering declaring it a celebration of our wonderful Planet instead. After all, it's been around a lot longer than I have, and no doubt it will still be here when I am long gone."

"Very fitting, Zohar," the Professor agreed.

"Well, it was a pleasure to meet you all and I'll see you at the celebrations. Norman, perhaps you could show me out?"

Norman led the way obediently. Spong trotted behind, hoping for a walk. On seeing the front door, he ran around and around the Master Poggle until he became entangled in the hem of Zohar's long robes. Norman hurriedly bent to free him. In doing so he noticed the Master's feet, which were usually covered by his flowing cloak. His middle toes were much longer than the others...

"Master! You're a—"

"Yes, Norman, you are not alone; but let's keep this a secret between ourselves, shall we?"

Rumours were spreading fast. Norman was used to Poggles pointing and whispering about him, but today felt different. The Zube Tubes were still out of action so the old tunnels were crowded, and the walk to the school pod was punctuated with hushed comments as they passed.

"... went to the Dark Side..."

"... Professor Zube is back..."

"... fought off ten Drones all by himself!"

"... that's his friend Ernie..."

Norman and Ernie felt themselves colour with embarrassment and hurried on. They were relieved when the attention was drawn away from them as Bert Snatchitt popped out of the Zube Tube next to the school pod looking very worse for wear.

"What on the Planet...?" he exclaimed as Poggles all around him held their hooters and stepped back. "The Zubes are full of dung! Who's done this?"

"Bert," Chief Warden Faircop bustled forward, "didn't you get the notice not to use the Zubes?"

"I most certainly did not!" Bert was outraged.

"I wonder how you got missed out?" Flint Zippo asked, aiming a sly wink at Norman and Ernie.

"Oh dear, Bert! What a mess... Here, come inside and let's get you cleaned up." Miss Lastic stepped out of the crowd proffering a totally inadequate lace hanky.

"Do stop fussing, Lucy," he grumbled, but reluctantly followed her.

Ernie burst out laughing.

"Poor Bert," said Norman. "Still, at least we'll be able to smell him coming for a while."

"Yes. That's not what I'm laughing at, though! It's Miss Lastic – her name's Lucy!"

"And?" Norm couldn't help smiling at his hysterical friend but he wasn't sure what was so funny.

"Think about it... Lucy Lastic!"

Ernie had just about recovered by the time school started. Miss Lastic was unusually late arriving and was met with pandemonium as everyone crowded round Norm, firing questions at him. Eventually she settled the class, only to lose control again as a message arrived confirming that the following day was to be a Planet-wide holiday concluding with a ceremony and party in the Star Chamber. Norman and Ernie grinned at each other as their classmates cheered.

"Well done, Norman!" Jeli Mould actually planted a kiss on his cheek as she congratulated him!

"Don't know what you two are smiling at," Boris hissed at them. "You might be flavour of the month today but I'll be the one they're talking about after my solo tomorrow!"

Ernie came down to the Planet with a bump as he remembered his disappointment. Norman watched his friend shuffle over to the insect care area and forlornly set about his feeding duties. An idea formed in his head. Checking to make sure no one was looking, Norman snuck over to the shelves of jam jars and slipped something from one of them into Boris's bubble bag.

"The holiday's not till tomorrow and we still have work to do today," Miss Lastic said wearily. "Now quiet down and boot up your Data-Globes... Select screen two thousand and seventy-four... Any questions?"

"Yes, Miss." Ernie's hand was raised as he stood by the insect tanks. "Could Fred be a girl's name?"

"What?" Miss Lastic was exasperated. "Not usually – why?"

"Well, then, we need a new name for Fred cos she's had babies!"

Uproar broke out again, led by Miss Lastic this time as she and the class crowded over to the Baracs Beetles' tank. Sure enough, Fred and Ginger were now the proud parents of seven miniature replicas of themselves, all waving their antennae hungrily.

"But... Well, I just assumed we'd been given a boy beetle when I was told it was called Fred!" Miss Lastic looked puzzled. "I was certain..."

"Well, one thing is certain," whooped Ernie, "we're gonna need a lot more dung!"

Miss Lastic threw her head back and laughed.

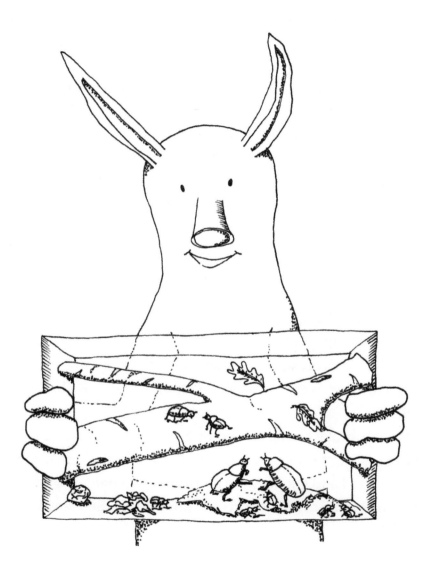

"We're gonna need a lot more dung!"

HOOTING WITH HONOURS

THE STAR CHAMBER had never looked so stunning.

Flint Zippo had been up all night hanging hundreds of extra jars of Firelighters, and their gleam was reflected in the eyes of every creature on the Planet as they crammed into the hall.

Norman tried to find a seat to one side, out of view, but had been steered to a bench right at the front by none other than Ilona Quinn. Moments later she escorted his mother, father and Spong to join him, and there they sat, self-consciously adjusting their best hats.

Underneath Norman's seat, eight glittering eyes reflected the Firelighters' glow as Scheherazade peeped out, taking care not to be seen – she wasn't going to miss *this*.

At least I can see Ernie from here, Norman thought to himself, and he smiled at his friend in the Hooting Choir nearby. Miss Harmony was busy handing out sheet music and conducting a last-minute tune-up. From his seat, Norm saw Boris Whinge arrive, looking puffed.

"Biss Harbody! Biss Harbody!" Boris gasped. "I've got a code id by dose ad I card blay!"

"Oh Boris, how did you catch that? You were fine yesterday."

"I dode know... bud I foud a Sneezewort id by bubble bag... Sub-one must hab pud id dere."

Ernie looked across at Norman. His friend shrugged innocently.

"Well, we don't want you spreading your germs here. You'd better go and sit with your family. Ernie, do you think you can manage the solo instead?"

"No problemo!" grinned Ernie, giving the thumbs-up sign to Norman.

A few moments later a bell tinkled, silence fell and Ernie raised his snout. The Chamber was filled with a single pure note, which grew in volume, filling every space with liquid joy. The note became a cascade of melodic trills as wave after wave of sound washed around the room, and echo built upon echo to a glorious crescendo. Then, just as it seemed as if the room could hold no more, the single pure note shone through again, clearing the air, until it too faded to nothing.

There was a brief moment of silence as Ernie lowered his snout and looked to the floor, and then the Chamber erupted in tumultuous applause and whistles. Poor Ernie glowed with embarrassment as Miss Harmony shook his hand proudly.

Gradually the applause died away until just one person remained clapping. Everyone turned their attention to the back of the hall to where the Master Poggle was standing.

He walked through the crowd towards Ernie, shook his hand and said, "Greetings, fellow Poggles, and be seated. I have a story to tell you about a Planet in peril. This Planet faces two dangers: one from without and one from within..." Murmurs of concern rippled around the room and Zohar raised his hand. "But fear not, this tale has an exceedingly happy ending and, unlike most stories, any similarity to living persons and real events is entirely intentional." The murmurs turned to laughter.

And so Zohar began to unfold the story that Norman and Ernie knew so well. The tension in the Chamber rose as, one by one, Poggles began to understand how close they had come to invasion by their old enemy the Drones. Panic broke out at the point where Zohar related Professor Zube's plan and the Professor himself entered from the wings of the stage, dwarfing his audience. They were soon calmed as Zohar embraced him warmly, and hoots of appreciation were heard.

"I must pause here," Zohar raised his hand for silence, which fell immediately, "to thank my dear friend and bestow upon him the Star of Wisdom for his Services to Science." He nodded towards Ilona Quinn, who handed him a ribbon of the palest golden yellow. The Professor bowed and took a seat on an empty table at the side of the stage.

Norman and Ernie squirmed with embarrassment as the Master continued narrating and their own part in the tale became clear. Nearby Poggles began nudging them and patting them on the back.

The Master paused again as he reached the point where Spong was stung by the Drone's tail. Some of the younger Poggles in the room began crying and had to be comforted, until Zohar called Spong onto the stage. Norman was delighted to see him rewarded with a Rosette for Bravery. Spong bounced happily around, drawing 'ahhs' from the crowd.

His mother was next and she found herself overwhelmed to receive the Star of Compassion 'for Services to Medicine and Tea Making'. She curtseyed gracefully as Zohar pinned a pale blue ribbon to her hat.

"And here is something more practical for you." Zohar reached into his pocket and produced four golden wheels. "I understand the casters from your tea trolley have gone missing, and we can't have that!"

As the laughter died away, Zohar continued in a more serious voice. Now he began to reveal the true extent of the deadly toxic waste problem. He left no detail out, much to Norman's shame when everyone laughed at his exploding hoover moment.

"Here I must pause again to bestow another honour, on a man of wise words and timely actions... Arthur Snodgrass, would you come forward to receive the Star of Wisdom?"

Norman rose to his feet with the rest of the Chamber and hooted loudly as his father bowed to receive his pale golden ribbon.

"You have proved yourself to be a Master of Mechanics, and I understand there is nothing you can't do with a bit of old wire?" Arthur Snodgrass nodded and obligingly produced a piece from under his hat.

"I therefore have a request to make of you. The Professor could use an extra pair of hands to upgrade the Zube Tube network. There is also the matter of modifying the waste-pipe system as I am delighted to report that we have a new generation of Baracs Beetles to feed!" A fresh cheer went up at this news.

"Professor Zube has some plans to create underground outlets to replace the Waste Dome. This will ensure a supply of fresh dung and eliminate the problem of toxic waste buildup in future. We would be delighted if you would accept the title of Chief Engineer and assist him."

Norman didn't hear his father's reply above the hooting in the Chamber but he watched with delight as Zohar handed him a pair of golden fine-nosed pliers.

"And now to bring our tale to its conclusion… It started with two friends… Norman, Ernie… would you join me, please?" Now the hooting was combined with the thunder of hundreds of Poggle feet as Norman and Ernie shuffled shyly onto the stage.

"You have heard their incredible story and know how we are all indebted to them. So, on behalf of all here, I would like to present Ernie with the Star of Loyalty for being a true friend in need…" He handed Ernie a purple ribbon.

Mrs Sludgebucket wiped tears from her eyes as she proudly announced to those around, "That's my son!"

"I would also like to commend him for his fine Services to Hooting!" Another cheer erupted followed by a loud sneeze from Boris Whinge.

"Finally, Norman… you have shouldered an immense burden and faced adversity with courage beyond your years. I know you doubted yourself along the way but, with the support of your family and friends, you shone through and proved yourself to be a brave and humble Warrior. It is only right that we give you the highest honour on our Planet – the Lightwise Star!"

With that, Zohar handed him the most beautiful crystal he had ever seen. With its many fine points reflecting thousands of jars of Firelighters, it seemed to be made of light itself. It was attached to a deep scarlet ribbon, exactly the same colour as Spong's fur… Norman's heart missed a beat. Why was Spong red?

A terrified cry from a Poggle at the side of the stage alerted him to the cause, as a deadly Drone emerged from the shadows.

The fifth member of the Landing Party had been hiding deep in the tunnels since the explosion on the Dark Side which had destroyed its home. Now desperation had forced it to overcome its fear of the light. Enraged at seeing the cause of its misery standing before it, it launched itself at Norman.

Strangely, it wasn't this but the sight of a black Scudder racing towards the stage that shocked Norman into action.

He yelped and stumbled backwards, throwing his hands up to shield himself. As he did so, the Lightwise Star was flung from his grasp. It soared high into the air, sparkling as if on fire, and then plunged towards the Drone. Silently, the sharpest point of the Star struck the Drone in the heart. At the same moment, Scheherazade sank her fangs deep into the Drone's up-reared tail.

The Drone gave a last cry of anguish and collapsed at Norman's feet.

Panic now erupted in the Chamber as Poggles ran in all directions. There was a dangerous crush at the back of the hall. Some of the Poggle Wardens were blowing their whistles while trying to guide the crowd to the exits. Bert Snatchitt, however, was shoving Poggles out of his way in an attempt to leave by the nearest Zube Tube.

A pure, piercing note rose above the chaos. One by one, the Poggles turned to see where it was coming from. On stage, the seven Elders had encircled the body of the Drone and their heads were lifted in song. As they hooted, they raised their arms until their cloaks hid the awful carcass from view. Moments later they stopped, lowered their arms – and the body was gone.

"Be calm, fellow Poggles – the danger has passed," Zohar soothed. "Once again, Norman has saved the day!"

Now the crush was at the front of the Chamber as the Poggles surged forward. Norman felt himself rise above the crowd as he was carried aloft on unknown shoulders, hats and flowers whizzing past his ears. The noise was deafening but wonderful.

To his left, he saw his dearest friend Ernie also being paraded around the Chamber, his grin only just contained by his face. They caught each other's eye and waved.

Below him, his parents hugged each other and looked up with proud, smiling eyes. On the stage, the Elders stood and clapped furiously. Now the same height as Professor Zube, their eyes met and the Professor bowed and saluted. Beside the Professor, Zohar held Spong and laughed as he ducked his licks.

*"Norm felt himself
rise above the crowd…"*

But in the rapturous chaos of the Star Chamber, one small creature was quiet and still in the shadows at the side of the stage. Nonetheless joyful, Scheherazade hid from view lest she be trodden on in the crush.

She looked on contentedly with her eight shining eyes.

Now, that, she thought, *was a tale worth telling.*

Norman Snodgrass will return in…

NORMAN SNODGRASS

OVER THE MOON